The Shadow of Mordican

THE LLANDOR TRILOGY
by Louise Lawrence

JOURNEY THROUGH LLANDOR
THE ROAD TO IRRIYAN
THE SHADOW OF MORDICAN

ANDRA
MOONWIND
WARRIORS OF TAAN
CHILDREN OF THE DUST

THE SHADOW OF MORDICAN

LOUISE LAWRENCE

Collins
An imprint of HarperCollins*Publishers*

First published in Great Britain by Collins 1996
1 3 5 7 9 10 8 6 4 2

Collins is an imprint of
HarperCollins*Publishers*Ltd,
77-85 Fulham Palace Road,
Hammersmith, London W6 8JB

ISBN 0 00 185648 0

The author asserts the moral right to be
identified as the author of this work.

A CIP record for this title is available
from the British Library.

Set in Stempel Garamond
Printed and bound in Great Britain by
Caledonian International Book Manufacturing Ltd, Glasgow G64

Asgaroth
R. ASGAR
Giants' Stairs
Northern Marches
Elandril
The Kellsfell
Kellswater
IRRIYAN
Greenlea
Kellsdale
The Western Havens
R. AVAR
Avaron
Scurry
R. SCURRY
Cape of Storms
Seers' Keep

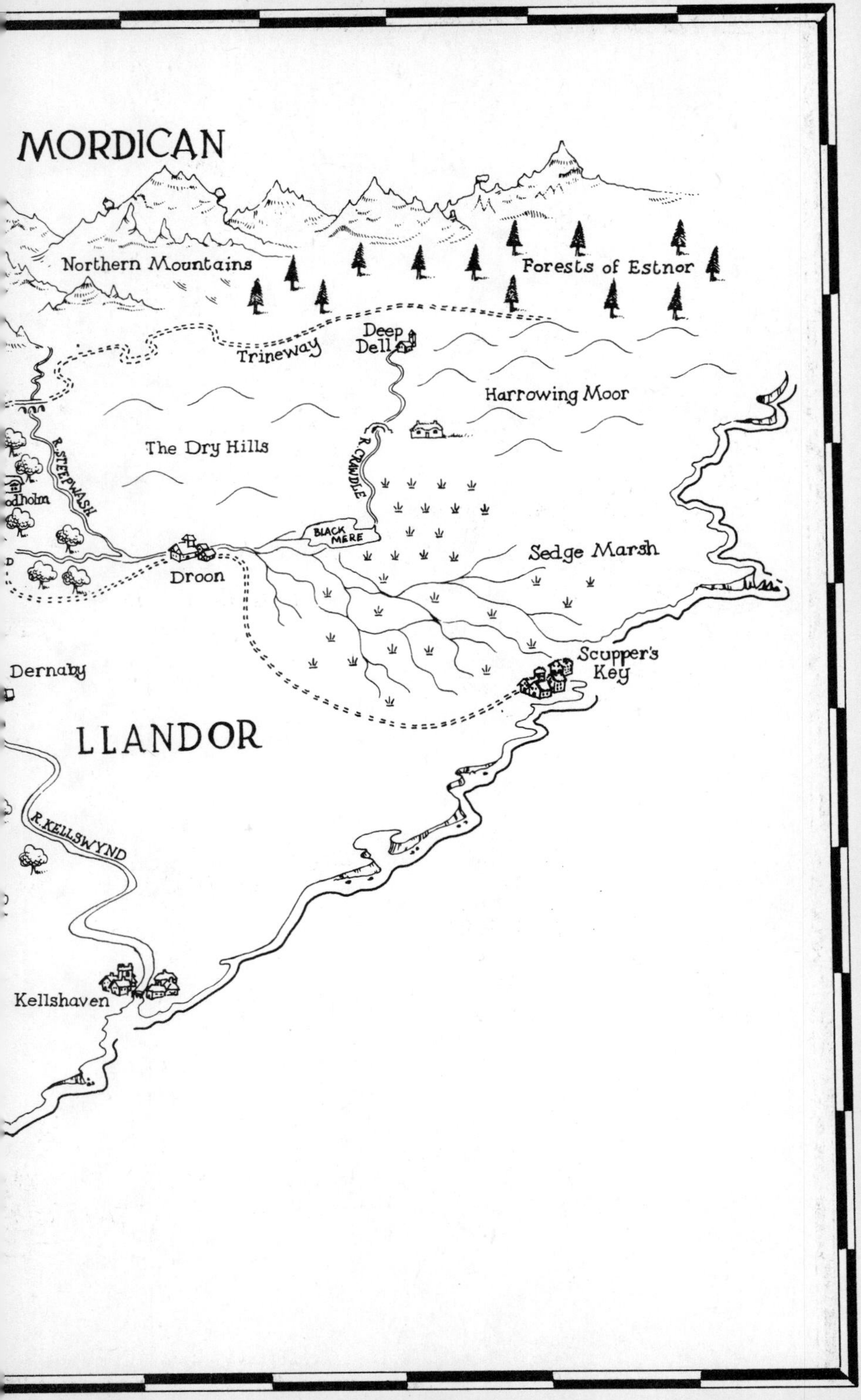

MORDICAN
Northern Mountains
Forests of Estnor
Deep Dell
Trineway
Harrowing Moor
The Dry Hills
R. STEEPWASH
R. CRAWDLE
odholm
BLACK MERE
Sedge Marsh
Droon
Scupper's Key
Dernaby
LLANDOR
R. KELLSWYND
Kellshaven

CHAPTER ONE

Kadmon the Black Mage stood alone on the ridge of the Kellsfell, his tattered robes fluttering in the wind that whined round the heights. Perched among the rocks some distance away, Craig watched him, heedless of the others sitting nearby. Kadmon's stillness was unnerving, as if he were not in his body at all but somewhere else. It was not impossible. He was a sorcerer, a flesh-sharer, able to escape from the confines of his skin whenever he willed. Glancing up, Craig saw a hawk wheeling and crying in the blue overhead sky, sensed Kadmon's presence casting its shadow on the lands beneath, and shivered in spite of the late afternoon sun.

The Black Mage terrified him and always had,

ever since he had attached himself to their company. He accessed a power that had long ago ceased to exist in the world Craig came from, wielded an arcane magic that had saved their lives on more than one occasion. Now, possessed by some foul entity Jerrimer called a soul-eater, driven to kill the wolf that had befriended Carrie and Janine, and betray Craig's whereabouts to the forces of the Grimthane that pursed him, Kadmon was even more dangerous.

It was Craig the Grimthane wanted, the knowledge in his head brought from his own world into this one. Ever since he, Carrie and Roderick came to Llandor they had been on the run, as had all those who travelled with them – elves and dwarfs and Gwillym the Mapper. It was Craig's surrender the rock trolls had demanded when they attacked the dwarven stronghold of Stonehast. But Roderick had bleached his hair and taken his place, gone with Diblin and an escort of trolls over the mountains to Mordican, leaving Craig to flee like a craven coward.

The memory galled him. He had never liked Roderick. And just because Kadmon had reached the Kellsfell before the rest of them did not necessarily mean the Black Mage was innocent. He'd had the opportunity and could have set things up with the rock trolls first. Craig was about to argue the point when Carrie rose to her feet. Tears trickled down her cheeks and her voice sounded desperate, her words echoing across the mountain slopes.

"I take it all back!" she cried. "Kadmon? Do you hear me? I take it all back!"

The Black Mage neither moved nor turned his head. Only the bird mewled sadly above him until finally Carrie turned on her heel, went running and scrambling across the scree. Her long plum-coloured skirt of woven wool tangled around her ankles and her silvery cloak billowed behind her, reflecting the shades of the sky and land in a muted camouflage of brown and grey and blue. Her hobnail boots, fashioned by the dwarfs of Deep Dell, clattered among the stones. It was the last Craig saw of her for a while, a girl with wild chestnut hair whom he had known all his life, vanishing among the golden mists that concealed the elven land of Irriyan from his sight.

"What was all that about?" asked Craig.

"Private between them?" suggested Gwillym.

It was another way of telling Craig to mind his own business and coming from Gwillym it was only to be expected. He and Craig had clashed before on several issues. Long-haired and bearded, Gwillym too had come from Craig's world but not from the same time. He had been a student at Bangor University in the 1960s when the values of society had been different and, having spent the last five years wandering through Llandor, Gwillym thought he knew everything and invariably took the lead.

"So what are we going to do about him?" Craig demanded.

"Who?" asked Gwillym.

"Kadmon," said Craig. "He can't come with us, can he?"

"I imagine he knows that," Janine said curtly.

Craig glanced towards where she sat with Jerrimer on a boulder. Flaxen hair, slanting brows and clear blue eyes marked them both as elven. They had been his friends once, Janine especially, ever since he, Carrie and Roderick blundered through the doorway in the woods and found themselves in Llandor. Keera, her mother, had taken them in, given them shelter in Woodholm before they set out on their journey to Seers' Keep. And Jerrimer, whom Craig had met in the Boar's Head tavern in Droon, had taught him to fish and handle a boat. But Janine, like Carrie, had grown to despise him and Jerrimer had not been the same since Maeve died in Sedge Marsh at the hands of the nixies.

Craig shrugged his indifference. He did not need anyone's friendship and Janine, at least, had confirmed what he suspected. No evil could enter the elven land and the flesh-sharer that dwelled within Kadmon's body was evil, a servant of the Grimthane. When they crossed the border into Irriyan, the Black Mage would not be going with them. With luck,

Craig and Kadmon would never meet again and Craig, for one, would have no regrets about that. He stared towards the golden mists where Carrie had gone.

"So what are we waiting for?" he asked.

With a sigh, Gwillym rose to his feet and picked up his backpack. And the others followed suit, except for the two dwarfs, Grifflin and Bannock. Grifflin, grey-bearded and elderly and almost as irascible as Diblin, and Bannock – a younger cheerier dwarf – had accompanied them from the rout of Stonehast and spent long days tramping through the mist and rain across the upland bogs to bring them safely to the Kellsfell. Now, so close to the borders of the elven land, they seemed reluctant to go further.

"Are you not coming with us?" asked Janine.

"I might," said Bannock, "after a while."

"Irriyan's no place for dwarfs," Grifflin said gruffly.

"Who says that?" asked Jerrimer. "As one who was born there I can assure you you will both be welcome."

"It's not the welcome that worries me," said Grifflin. "It's the land itself. Soft it is and addles one's brains, or so I've heard. All right for elves, perhaps, but we dwarfs are made of tougher stuff. We'll return to our mountain stronghold where we belong, thanking you kindly, sir elf."

"Is that what you say, too?" Janine asked Bannock.

"I've yet to decide," Bannock informed her.

"Now you listen to me…" Grifflin began.

Bannock grinned.

"Don't try to dissuade me, Grifflin. I know what you're about. Dwarfs for the dwarfs is all very well but where does it get us? We're cut off from the rest of Llandor without a say in anything. Maybe it's time we broadened our horizons and forged an alliance with Seers' Keep before it's too late. Against rock trolls and goblins and the darkness of Mordican, we have stood alone long enough."

"Dwarfs will never yield to Seers' Keep!" growled Grifflin.

"Rather the Seers than the Grimthane!" Bannock retorted.

"That makes sense," said Craig. "If you're militarily isolated then you're asking to get attacked."

"And in Llandor, no one is yielding to anyone!" Gwillym argued. "Serfdom has been outlawed here ever since the defeat of the giants! You should be knowing that, Grifflin. And if you are coming with us, Bannock, you will please to be making up your mind. It will be sundown in less than an hour."

Bannock nodded, and rose to join them. "I may as well," he said.

Grifflin scowled and shook his grizzled head.

"No good will come of it, young Bannock. You'll turn into a milksop the minute you enter Irriyan, you mark my words!"

Janine chuckled and cupped her hands.

"Kadmon! We're going!" the elf girl called.

But again from the Black Mage there was no response, only the bird soaring above him, his sorcerer's soul riding the wind currents, watching and waiting.

"Leave him be," Gwillym advised.

They turned in a body, and set their faces towards Irriyan, the gold light that beckoned them on. Grifflin accompanied them, determined to go as far as the border. Craig did not know what prompted him to look back – the scream of the hawk, perhaps, as it dropped like a stone beyond the ridge of the Kellsfell and became the scream of a man. Kadmon had gone from the edge on which he had been standing. Now nothing remained but the wind and the sunlight, a sense of loss and the brightness dimming. And something flashed past him, a blink of dark that streaked away northwards.

"What on earth was that?" Craig exclaimed.

The others seemed frozen, dark silhouettes where the bright mists began, then one by one they turned and came hurrying back towards him.

"Did you hear—?" said Craig.

"I heard," Gwillym said grimly.

"Someone screamed," said Jerrimer.

"A death cry," muttered Grifflin.

"And where's Kadmon?" asked Janine.

"He just disappeared," said Craig.

Bannock, on his stocky legs, was already running along the ridge towards the ledge where Kadmon had been standing, and the others followed, Craig at the rear, still bemused by what he had seen and felt and unsure of the implications. And the sense of absence seemed to spread like ripples from a pool, sweeping outwards in all directions, growing and intensifying as if the land mourned.

Imagination, thought Craig, yet the feeling remained. On the north horizon the far mountains brooded and, eastwards, the miles of bog over which he had travelled exuded a sadness. There was a chill in the sunlight and, southwards, the shadow of the Kellsfell stretched long and dark over the valley beneath.

It was Jerrimer's sharp elven eyes that spotted Kadmon's body lying on the scree slope maybe three hundred metres below. And the hawk, which had borne his soul through the last moments of life, was perched on the branch of a stunted rowan above him, its plaintive mewling echoing from the stone of the cliff over which Kadmon had fallen, as if it, too, mourned.

"So he's finally done it," Gwillym murmured.

"Roderick said he might," muttered Jerrimer.

"Dead," sobbed Janine.

"I reckon," Bannock said glumly.

"But we don't know for sure!" argued Craig. "We thought he was dead once before, drowned in the underground lake, but he wasn't!"

Grifflin shook his head. As a dwarven warrior he had seen his share of slaughter and was not given to hoping in the face of facts. "No one could have survived that fall," he stated.

"So what made him fall?" Craig asked hotly. "The wind's not that strong—"

"He was choosing it," said Gwillym.

"How do you mean?" asked Craig.

"He jumped," Jerrimer said quietly.

"Why would he—?"

"He had no alternative," sobbed Janine. "It was the only thing he could do, the only way he could escape from it."

"Escape from what?" asked Craig.

"The soul-eater," said Jerrimer.

"No use to a flesh-sharer is a dead body," said Gwillym.

Craig froze as he remembered. It had actually passed him, a blink of dark arrowing northwards, a formless entity evicted from Kadmon's corpse at the moment of impact, the moment of dying. Unbound, it would return to Mordican, one of the Grimthane's minions knowing all the Black Mage had known: that Craig had escaped from Stonehast and the rock trolls had captured Roderick by mistake. And how long would it take for the Grimthane to muster his forces in yet another pursuit? For the goblin hordes to cross the mountains, or Merrigan's army of crows to take flight? Already the yellow mists, which marked the boundary between Llandor and Irriyan, dimmed as the sun began to sink and the shadow of the Kellsfell darkened as a shroud round Kadmon's body.

"We've got to leave!" Craig said urgently.

"We can hardly leave yet," Gwillym objected. "That is Kadmon down there! We are owing him a decent burial at least!"

"We don't have time for that!" said Craig.

Gwillym clenched his fists. His grey eyes flashed and there was a steely edge to his voice. "Without Kadmon to lead us it is falling on me, not you, to say what must be done!" he announced. "Surely, even raised in the 1990s, you cannot be so lacking in respect—"

"You don't understand!" said Craig.

"Nor you!" Jerrimer said coldly. "As Kadmon did for Maeve so I will do for him! There is time enough before sundown to build a cairn of stones. I owe him that much!"

"So do we all," said Janine.

"What about the flesh-sharer?" Craig demanded.

"What about it?" asked Gwillym.

"I felt it! I saw it! It passed me! And it headed north! A blink of dark, Gwillym! By now the Grimthane could know where we are! If we spend another night on the Kellsfell we could be caught! And if that happens Kadmon's death will be pointless, won't it? We've got to go, don't you see? We've got to catch up with Carrie, cross the border into Irriyan! We've got no choice!"

Evening shadows deepened and their faces darkened as, one by one, they turned to scan the sky above the northern mountains. Strange clouds massed around the high pass into Mordican and flickers of lightning played about the snowy peaks. Briefly Craig wondered how Roderick fared, whether his subterfuge had been discovered and whether or not he was still alive, but his thoughts fled in a renewed sense of urgency.

"We've got to go!" he insisted.

"He's right," said Jerrimer reluctantly.

"But we can't leave Kadmon!" wailed Janine.

"Me and Bannock will take care of him," said Grifflin.

"Do what must be done," confirmed Bannock.

"I thought you were coming with us?" said Gwillym.

"Maybe I'll catch you up," said Bannock. "Or maybe I won't. Maybe I'll travel my own way at my own speed, or maybe I'll see Grifflin safely back to Stonehast. But you go, all of you. Whatever's in those clouds is none too friendly."

He uncoiled the length of rope from round his waist, tied one end to the staff he carried and wedged it between two rocks. Then he threw the loose end over the ledge and made to descend.

"I am not knowing what to say," Gwillym murmured.

Craig turned away. Leave-takings could last all night and it was not really the dwarfs they were parting from, but Kadmon. And however much Craig had feared the Black Mage, he was more afraid without him, knowing he was exposed and vulnerable, deprived of his protective powers. The clouds above the northern mountains lowered. Their lightnings menaced and, without waiting for the others, Craig wrapped the silvery elven cloak closer round himself and set out across the scree slope after Carrie.

The bright mists soon hid him from Llandor. The land he had hated from the moment he set foot in it was behind him then, and all the horrors it contained. Boggart-infested marshes, rivers where flesh-eating kelpies lay in wait, underground caverns guarded by rock worms, armies of crows and the wraiths of Harrowing Moor, all rose in his memory, faded and were gone. Now mist only remained, swirling round him like smoke made of sunlight, as if some bright beautiful beacon shone beyond it and led him on.

He knew he was still on the ridge of the Kellsfell. He could see the rocks and stones around him, the scree gilded like gold, and crags up ahead of him shining in the strange opaque light. Yet Llandor was gone in every other sense. It was as if nothing existed beyond the limits of his sights and hearing: no world, no time, no sound, no wind nor weather, no human voices. It was as if nothing could penetrate the barrier of light and silence that separated Llandor from Irriyan. Even his own footsteps seemed muffled.

It might have been frightening, a total disconnection from all that had been there a few moments before, but fear was something else that no longer existed. Craig did not know why, but he knew he was safe, shielded from everything that threatened him. Even the air, which had chilled with the approach of evening on the heights of the Kellsfell, grew moist and warm as if he were entering a different world, a different climate. The mist swirled and thickened and the light grew brighter. Gold drops of moisture beaded his cloak, danced in the emptiness around him, sparkled like airborne diamonds and dazzled his eyes.

Faint and far away in the distance behind him he heard voices calling a name he failed to recognise as his own, and somewhere ahead he heard the sound of tumbling water. He walked towards it and the sound increased until finally he saw a river pouring over a sheer ledge into a chasm full of rainbows. The noise was deafening and how deep it was he did not know and could not guess, although maybe he would soon find out.

Before him a slender bridge arched through the light, a single fragile span that seemed to lead from nowhere into nowhere. Unafraid, Craig began to cross it, clutching the handrail that guarded the abyss beneath. Blue and white, the thundering torrent fell through the spaces, but the bottom of the falls remained unseeable, and the spume and spray of the nameless river, the source of the ever-rising mist, faded quite suddenly as he stepped from the bridge and emerged into the evening in Irriyan.

Unreal as a dream, perfect and beautiful, the elven land spread out before him. Under a sky rosy with sunset, purple shade and indigo shadows spread across an undulating countryside of woods and fields and rolling hills. Sapphire mountains straddled the far horizon and a myriad fairy lights, small as the overhead stars, winked in the darkening valleys. Nearby, a sloping meadow spangled with flowers led down to an orchard frothy with blossoms and loud with nightingales. Apple blossom and birdsong and a thousand other scents and sounds and sights mingled with the music of the waterfall into a single perception of life that stunned Craig's senses. All he could do was stand and stare, breathe and experience it, enthralled by Irriyan's magic.

"Isn't it wonderful?" murmured Carrie.

She was sitting on the grass beneath the spreading branches of a tree. Leaves gilded by autumn, ruffled by a warm breeze from the south, drifted groundwards although it was spring or summer in the land below. The fallen leaves rustled beneath Craig's feet as he moved to sit beside her. She seemed glad to see him, smiled as she had in school at Lydminster before they came to Llandor and she grew to hate him.

He remembered it clearly for a moment – how Carrie had changed, rejecting the world she came from and not wanting to return there, rejecting him, too, and all he believed in. Throughout their journey she had seldom missed an opportunity to humiliate or undermine him. Yet it seemed not to matter any more. It was part of the past along with everything else in Llandor. Gazing into Carrie's grey eyes, Craig knew he would forget everything, forgive everything, as long they stayed in Irriyan.

He brushed aside the unruly curls from Carrie's face. He did not want to tell her, but someone had to.

"Kadmon's dead," he said gently.

She did not cry as he expected. She did not seem to react at all, except that her smile faded and her eyes went blank. Emotionless, she turned her gaze to the twilit land, listened without comment as Craig told her what had happened. Kadmon had died, and strange how long ago it seemed and how far away, something that had occurred in another time and another world, remote from both of them. Or maybe grief was something else that could not exist in Irriyan, and death became meaningless in the midst of so much life.

The nightingales sang on in spite of it. The stars shone brighter and the flowers released their scents and a dozen white horses, some with riders on their back wearing scarlet cloaks and carrying lanterns on poles, came cantering up the grassy slope towards them. Proud horses, Craig noted, with dainty steps, their white manes flowing and a single horn rising from their foreheads. Unicorns, no less, and yet he could accept them without surprise, creatures of myth as real as he was, as real as Janine, Jerrimer and Gwillym who suddenly emerged from the river-mists behind him.

"So we are finally making it," Gwillym murmured.

"Home," Jerrimer said simply.

"Irriyan, where my mother was born!" breathed Janine.

"Isn't it wonderful?" Carrie repeated.

"Have you told her of Kadmon?" Gwillym asked Craig.

"He's dead," Carrie said matter-of-factly. "And are those really unicorns coming towards us?"

Jerrimer looked where she pointed and quietly whistled. "If they've sent out the unicorn riders they must be expecting someone important."

Gwillym glanced at the mists behind him, white and pale with starshine now the sunset had faded. "I wonder who?" he murmured.

The riders approached, drew in their mounts, and the unicorns on the leading reins halted beside them. Elves, six of them altogether, and similar to Jerrimer, small and neat with flaxen hair and pointed ears, leapt lightly to the ground. Their scarlet cloaks and tunics gleamed in the light of their moonstone lanterns. Gold insignia shone on their shoulders and their blue eyes glowed.

"Well come," said one. "Delbeth has sent us to meet you."

"Us?" said Gwillym.

"Your coming was foreseen," the elf replied.

"But one of you is missing," said another.

"Kadmon is dead," Carrie said airily.

The elves glanced at each other.

"If one of you is missing it is not for that reason," their spokesman said. "Delbeth foresaw no death. Six, she saw, and six spare mounts have we brought. There should be a dwarf."

"You mean Bannock?" said Gwillym. "He stayed

behind to help Grifflin bury Kadmon. He could be following us later, see?"

The elf turned to his companions. "I'll wait for him," he said, "at least until morning. You, Garriel, take these five to the elf-seer as she has requested."

Leading his own and one spare mount, he headed into the mist towards the boundary of his land, leaving the elf named Garriel in charge. Tethering the unicorns to a hazel bough, and unpacking their shoulder bags, the remaining elves set a makeshift supper on the grass: ripe fruit and cheese and wafer bread, and flasks of honey mead to quench their thirst.

"Eat," said Garriel. "It is a long journey back to Elandril."

"Who's Elandril?" asked Craig.

"Not a person but a place," said Gwillym.

"Irriyan's second city," said Jerrimer.

"Where my mother was born," added Janine.

"We're not actually going to ride a unicorn, are we?" asked Carrie.

"Now and then, when needs must, they consent to carry passengers," Garriel informed her.

"But I don't know how to ride!" Carrie protested.

Garriel chuckled. "Don't worry," he said. "We'll give you Shoshuna. She's less flighty than most and all you need do is sit astride her."

Craig, too, had never ridden before although,

woozy from the mead, he barely remembered the final departure. High on the unicorn's back, nervous at first, his knuckles clutching its rein growing white and tense, he headed away with the rest of them into the night. At first the land was no more than a blur of darkness on either side. Then, as his night-vision adjusted and his head cleared, he saw everything glowing with the luminescence of its own life. Grass blades glittered like glass, and every leaf was edged with an aura of gold, and the meadow flowers shone like multicoloured jewels – rubies, sapphires and amethysts that faded as he stared.

He looked back only once. The Kellsfell was a dark hump against the skyline and the mists, which rose from the chasm where the river plunged over its falls, hung as a wall of pale fog at its foot. It was the River Avar, said Gwillym who was riding beside him, and five hundred miles to the south was the port of Avaron from where they would set sail to Seers' Keep. Just for a moment Craig was aware of a mutinous feeling stirring within him, a wild sense of rebellion he was unable to fathom, but it faded when he turned his face towards Irriyan again and almost instantly he forgot.

The unicorns picked up speed and the night breezes blew through his hair. Voices, elven and human, laughed and chattered around him. Cloaks, scarlet and silver, swirled and billowed, and the moonstone lanterns cast their fragile light upon the land, vying with the shifting elusive auras of moths and owls, leaves and flowers, and small nocturnal creatures. No place for hate or anger or any other dark emotions. The magic of Irriyan drove them from his mind, and the antagonism that had existed between him and Gwillym was over. They were merely compatriots, two human beings come from the same world for the same unknown reason.

But it was worse for Gwillym, thought Craig. In the five years he had been in Llandor, thirty-five years had passed in the world he had come from. Everyone Gwillym had known in the 1960s had either grown old or died. Even if a doorway between the worlds should open now before them, Gwillym could not go back to Wales.

And for Craig himself the hope of ever returning to his home in Ditchford was fading. In the months since he, Carrie and Roderick had come to Llandor, several years might have passed. His future as a computer expert was slipping away with every moment he remained. Yet even that no longer seemed to matter, as if being in Irriyan was compensation enough for all he had lost. He could bear being exiled if he stayed in Irriyan, he thought, and he might even be glad.

"Have you been to Irriyan before?" he asked Gwillym.

"I have," said Gwillym.

"So why did you leave? Given a choice, I think I'd stay here for ever."

Eyes in the lantern light grey as the Welsh mountains of Gwillym's homeland regarded Craig and twinkled with suppressed mirth. "Under the spell already?" asked Gwillym. "That was quick. It is the air, some say. Acts like a drug, it does, until you get used to it. Then you begin to remember... your life has a purpose which is not in Irriyan, see?"

Craig frowned. He understood what Gwillym was saying, but what was true for him was not true for Craig. Elsewhere, in Llandor, Craig had no purpose but now he knew it was enough simply to live, providing that life was in Irriyan. And if the elven land *had* cast a spell on him he could only pray it would last for ever.

CHAPTER TWO

After several days of forced marching, through fog and rain and low cloud that obscured any glimpses of the land he was leaving, Roderick neared the top of the Giants' Stairs. His captors, the rock trolls, following after the Black Mage who led them, marched in gloomy silence, half a dozen on either side preventing his escape. He was used to them by now, towering craggy forms with shaggy hair, wearing coats and breeches that seemed to be woven out of tree bark, their grey faces scabbed with lichen. Each one carried a great stone club and their acid-yellow eyes peered short-sightedly at the rugged landscape through which they travelled.

The rock trolls failed to see what Roderick and

Diblin, the dwarf, saw quite clearly at times: two small goblin forms scuttling among the rocks and boulders on the slopes above them. Rikkin's round milk-white eyes watched from the shadows at nightfall, and sometimes they saw the tell-tale flash of scarlet that was Umla's hair ribbon bobbing across the barren scree. Roderick could not imagine why the goblins followed, yet their presence comforted almost as much the dwarf who marched beside him.

Diblin may have been tetchy even in the best of tempers, but to Roderick he was a staunch and trusted friend. And he had no need to ask why the dwarf went with him. Diblin owed Roderick his life, owed him for saving him from the boggarts on Black Mere and, bound by the dwarven code of honour, that debt had yet to be paid. And nothing Roderick could say would excuse him from it.

As for the sorcerer who led them and claimed to be Kadmon, he wore his hood pulled up against the weather and kept his face concealed. Glancing to neither left nor right, he tramped before them, keeping his eyes fixed firmly on the stepped road rising ahead. And when they camped at night he sat apart, his features hidden from the firelight. He had never once looked at Roderick. If he had, and he really was Kadmon, he would have realised long ago that Roderick was not Craig. But the omission confirmed what Roderick had suspected ever since they left Stonehast. Whoever wore those dark flowing robes was not the Black Mage.

"I'm sure he's an imposter," Roderick whispered.

"That's what you say!" muttered Diblin.

"The stance is wrong for Kadmon," said Roderick.

"The smell's the same," the dwarf declared.

"Are you absolutely sure about that, Diblin?"

"I know wizardry when I whiff it, boy."

"I'm not denying he's a sorcerer," said Roderick. "But which sorcerer? Even under the influence of the flesh-sharer Kadmon wouldn't side with the Grimthane for this length of time. He'd fight it, Diblin, and anyone can put on black robes and claim to be the Black Mage."

"He's still a sorcerer," the dwarf repeated.

"But if he was Kadmon he'd know me," Roderick insisted.

Diblin was silent for a moment. Moisture dewed his beard and bristling brows, and his dark deepset eyes looked thoughtful.

"So you reckon the rock trolls have been fooled in more ways than one?" he mused. "And how does that help us?"

"It doesn't," said Roderick. "Unless they find out, perhaps?"

Diblin looked at him in alarm.

"If you're thinking of telling them, boy, I'd advise you to forget it!" hissed the dwarf. "They're likely to brain the lot of us! You and me as well as the Black Mage!"

"Or they might just release us and turn on him," said Roderick. "It's worth a try, isn't it?"

Their voices were low, unheard above the lumbering tread of their captors. Ahead, the steps levelled out and the road wound on through a mountain pass flanked by high cliffs and hung with cloud. It was early evening. Roderick's legs ached from long hours of climbing and if he and Diblin were to risk making allies of the rock trolls, they had to do it now while they were still in Llandor. Tomorrow might be too late. By then they could be in Mordican, deep within the Grimthane's territory and beyond any hope of escape.

Roderick had tried not to think of what the Grimthane might do to him when he discovered his true identity, and what might be his eventual fate. When it came to physical pain he had never been brave. And now a quick fear filled him, gripped his stomach and loosened his bowels to the point of desperation.

"I need to go," he said loudly.

"Go where?" growled Diblin.

"To the lavatory," said Roderick.

The rock trolls halted. As with the goblin race, they all understood English well enough but not many of them spoke it. Their strange hooting language echoed around the heights, recalling the sorcerer who led them. Faceless in the gathering twilight, the man in black robes retraced his steps.

"Why the hold-up?" he snapped.

"We stop!" boomed the troll who had become the spokesman.

"There is light enough left for another league of marching!" the sorcerer retorted. "And if you would gain the Grimthane's protection for your lands, you had best get our prisoner to Asgaroth sooner rather than later."

"Our charge is to deliver him alive, not dead," the troll reminded him. "The boy has travelled far enough this day and has needs that must be met. We shall camp here tonight, sorcerer."

"Are you asking my permission, Dagda?"

"I'm informing you," Dagda replied calmly.

The sorcerer clenched his fists, then shrugged and turned away, clambering up the nearby scree slope to sit with his back to the company on a high outcrop of rock. And beneath the flowing blackness of his robes, Roderick caught a glimpse of some white garb. Whoever he was, he was not Kadmon, Roderick thought again. But the White Mage had gone missing, he remembered Jerrimer saying. So maybe it was he who engineered this masquerade?

Roderick did not know, and nor did he know what powers the unknown sorcerer might hurl against him if he should make a move. Gripping his stomach against the renewed stirrings of fear, wrapping his elven cloak tightly round himself to stave off the mountain's chill, and accompanied by two of the rock trolls who would stand guard nearby, he headed for the privacy of a sizeable boulder to relieve himself.

The remaining rock trolls, hooting softly to each other, set about emptying their backpacks, building a cook-fire with charcoal they had carried with them and preparing to feed their prisoners. Their luminous eyes were beginning to glow with pale yellow light as the daylight faded, and height and size made them intimidating. But although their enmity towards the dwarven race stretched back through the centuries, they had so far shown no violence either to Roderick or Diblin. Indeed, the one named Dagda had almost seemed to be defending Roderick against the sorcerer's demands. It had to be worth trying to gain their friendship, thought Roderick. Regardless of Diblin's beliefs, it had to be worth it.

Determinedly he rose and fastened his clothing, and was about to step forward and speak to the rock trolls guarding him when someone tugged sharply at the hem of his cloak. Unless he had caught it on something? He turned to find a pair of round pale eyes regarding him and pointy ears that pricked and stirred with every small sound. The creature's wide grin exposed a set of razor-sharp teeth.

"Umla?" whispered Roderick.

"You come with me!" the goblin-girl hissed.

"What for?" whispered Roderick.

"We escape now, back into Llandor."

"What about Diblin?"

"Rikkin bring dwarf. You come with me. Quickly, Roderick!"

Roderick did not stop to think. He followed her between the boulders. The cloak he wore, of elven fabric, melted into the greyness of the twilight and made him all but invisible, but his hobnail boots, cobbled by the dwarfs of Deep Dell, inevitably gave him away. Rock trolls were short-sighted, but they were neither deaf nor stupid. Stones, dislodged by Roderick's feet, rattled down the mountain slope, and loud hollering cries all too soon informed him he was being pursued.

Glancing over his shoulder he could see his guards, the eerie glow of their eyes and their massive grey shapes lumbering after him through the mist. And Umla, small and agile in her rabbit-skin clothes, was scuttling ahead of him. With splayed toes and clawed hands, she began to scale an almost vertical path upwards, forgetful of Roderick's size and limited human abilities. He knew it was impossible before he even began. He was neither athletic nor good at heights. One leap, one chance, was all he had – but his fingers failed to grip. He slithered back downwards to be caught and held by the stony hands of the trolls. Above him Umla uttered a small forlorn cry as Roderick was hauled back towards the camp, and the firelight, and the road to Mordican.

Diblin, bruised and bleeding from a cut on his forehead, lay spread-eagled on the hard ground with Dagda's foot on his stomach. And Rikkin, with fear stark in his eyes, his arms pinioned to his sides and his legs flailing, was held securely by another troll. Dampness dripped from Roderick's bleached hair as his captors pushed him forward into the ring of firelight where the sorcerer stood. Unseen eyes regarded him and the sorcerer's voice, when he finally spoke, was low and menacing.

"Try that again, Craig, and your friends will die. And you will be carried into Asgaroth, your mind at the mercy of my mind, your limbs unable to obey you."

Roderick swallowed, but now was not the time to betray his own fear. He shook off the hands that held him and faced the man boldly.

"Who's going to carry me?" he demanded. "The trolls? Why should they do that when they learn how they've been duped? I've spent months in the company of the Black Mage, and you're not him! And whatever you've told the trolls that has persuaded them to go along with you is probably untrue!"

There were hoots all around him, shrill, questioning, and indignant, and ire glowed in a dozen pairs of acid-yellow eyes. But the sorcerer raised his hands in a quick response and Roderick had no chance to capitalize on his advantage. His vocal cords seized up and his mind went blank, unable to think or reason. His legs, turned suddenly to the consistency of water, failed to support him. His body jarred as he hit the ground. Incapable of moving until the spell wore off, he lay with the impressions of stones indenting his flesh, feeling the throbbing pain of countless small hurts, listening to the howling, angry exchange of voices above him.

"The boy's right!" raged the dwarf. "I know the Black Mage, too, and that man's not him! He's a cheating imposter!"

"Kadmon go west!" shrieked Umla as she stepped into the circle of firelight. "Me and Rikkin see him go!"

"Is true! Is true!" squeaked Rikkin.

The troll named Dagda removed its foot from Diblin's stomach and the dwarf scrambled to his feet, gesticulating wildly. "Tell him to take off his hood and show us his face!" yelled Diblin.

"Take it off, sorcerer!" Dagda instructed.

Partially recovered, Roderick sat up.

And the Black Mage laughed.

"I obey no orders but the Grimthane's, rock troll! And if you listen to the likes of dwarfs and goblins, you are a fool indeed! We had an agreement! You deliver Craig to Asgaroth and the forces of Mordican will protect your territory in the Northern Marches—"

"Protect it from what?" Roderick demanded.

"Attack!" hissed the sorcerer.

"By dwarfs and elves," boomed Dagda. "They plan a massed assault on two of our borders, from Irriyan in the south and the dwarven strongholds in the east."

"Rubbish!" growled Diblin. "We dwarfs don't go looking for trouble! And there aren't enough of us left in the mountains to launch a massed assault! As for the elves – well, they forswore war centuries ago. I doubt if they even know *how* to fight! Elves and dwarfs have little truck with each other anyway! And we certainly haven't drawn up any battle plans between us! The man's a liar, plain and simple, if that's what he told you!"

Again the sorcerer raised his hands. Firelight glittered in a pair of ice-blue eyes that were fixed on Diblin. And Roderick was still feeling too battered to stand. He could only scream out his warning as Umla leapt. Goblin claws raked at the sorcerer's face, and the red bolt of lightning hurled from his fingertips shot wide of its mark, striking one of the trolls instead. The creature exploded. Stony fragments, that should have been Diblin's flesh, showered like rain in the darkness.

The trolls needed no more convincing. Whoever the sorcerer was, he was ruthless and dangerous, and one of their kind was dead. Releasing Rikkin, and heedless of Diblin and Roderick who were supposed to be their captives, they followed Umla's lead: a dozen rock trolls, minus one, about to attack and intending to still or restrain him.

Roderick witnessed then what powers the sorcerer possessed. The forces of nature obeyed him. Crackling red light blasted several trolls to dust before they even came near him. Two more vanished as a crack in the ground opened beneath them. Swirling clouds released a deluge of rain that sluiced down the Giants' Stairs from the mountain pass, extinguishing the camp fire, washing away boulders and the two goblins and the trolls' broken bodies, battering Roderick's face.

There was little he could do. He could only watch, helplessly, as Diblin floundered and fell. His cry of grief went unheard, drowned by the rain, and the brief tears were washed from his face. Numbed out of thought, he felt for a stone to throw as the water turned to ice in the blast of cold that followed.

The ground froze in seconds. The one troll that remained standing became a statue of ice in the darkness, a shape whitened with hoar frost and frozen where it stood, almost indistinguishable from the rocks and boulders around it. And the clouds cleared, revealing a sky bitter and bright with stars, an icy sheen of light over all things and a deathly silence. It was so cold Roderick could barely breath. He could feel the air in his lungs beginning to freeze. The sorcerer stood still, his black robes billowing in the arctic wind, his hood blown back and his features finally revealed. He was ginger-haired, ginger-bearded, his face pallid in the starlight. The blue pale eyes, that were not Kadmon's, regarded Roderick and his voice grated.

"Get up!" he commanded.

"I can't!" groaned Roderick.

The sorcerer snapped his fingers.

On Roderick's clothes the ice-film cracked. Small shards that glittered as glass fell from his cloak, and an eddy of warmth swirled around him.

His breathing eased. His limbs began to thaw. His toes and fingers throbbed with pain. He realised he could move again, and that in his hand he was clutching a sizeable stone. Too late to wish he really *was* Craig, good at sports and accurate with a cricket ball. All he could do was obey the sorcerer's instructions, struggle to his feet, silently pray and take aim.

The stone struck hard and the sorcerer fell. Hot tears of relief scalded Roderick's cheeks as he went to check on him. Dark blood trickled from a gash on his forehead, matted his hair and pooled in the closed sockets of his eyes. And yet again this land had driven Roderick to kill, not boggarts this time but a man. Or maybe not? A faint pulse indicated the sorcerer was still alive and might recover. Without emotion, Roderick unlaced the leather thongs that bound the legs of his own trousers, made a straitjacket of the sorcerer's robes and lashed him securely inside it. Then he rose to his feet to face the carnage that lay around him. Where there had been life in the mountains a moment ago there was now nothing but emptiness and silence. Yet more noticeable even than that was the huge sense of absence that came sweeping towards him, an ending elsewhere that even the stones seemed to feel. He turned his head. The night was not as dark as he had thought, the day not as late. Far in the west he could see a brightness in the sky and fiery streaks of sunset. Had they got there? he wondered. Had Craig and Carrie, Gwillym and Jerrimer reached the safety of Irriyan?

He thought, if he ran, he could maybe catch up with them, but he made no move to leave. The sadness gripped him, the grief of a land that mingled with his own renewed grief, as he took off his elven cloak and covered Diblin's frozen body. Squatting beside the dwarf who had been his friend, he was again aware of the horrifying effects of his, Craig's and Carrie's presence in Llandor. They were there for a purpose, Keera had said. And the land called who the land needed, Kadmon had declared. But so far all they had done was cause people to die who tried to protect them. Why? Roderick thought wretchedly. The sorcerer's death he could have borne but not Diblin's, nor Rikkin's and Umla's either.

He remembered seeing the two small goblins being swept away by the deluge, and began searching for their bodies among the rocks. The darkness deepened and, without his elven cloak, the night wind chilled him to the bone. And all he found were the smashed torsos and broken limbs of the rock trolls.

Even for them Roderick grieved, once-living creatures who had taken him captive and died because of it. One remained standing, its troll-shape turned to a pillar of ice, but the rest needed burying, and there was only him left to do it. Grimly, he began what would be for him a night-long task of shifting stones to cover their remains. Ice crunched beneath his boots, melted in places and runnelled away, and the clatter he made was loud in the unbroken silence until a hand on his shoulder caused him to yelp in sudden fright and drop the stone he carried.

"Leave it," murmured Dagda. "The dead are dead but the living come first. If you are to survive the night you need fire and warm food. We must search for the backpacks we carried. Some may contain tinder and charcoal, bread that might have escaped the drenching."

Roderick looked up. Icicles dripped from the rock troll's hair. It had thawed from its freezing and miraculously survived. Its acid-yellow eyes, luminous and shining, gazed down on him and reflected his own grief. It had feelings too, he realised, thoughts and emotions and a mind capable of its own kind of logic. It mourned the loss of its companions as much as he mourned, yet at the same time it considered the needs of one human youth who had survived.

"You're going to help me?" Roderick asked it.

"We'll help each other," Dagda replied.

"We should have done that at Stonehast," Roderick said bitterly.

"Co-operation is something all races need to learn," Dagda said sadly. "And with hindsight it is easy to be wise."

Cold and shivering, Roderick accompanied the rock troll in its search among the rocks. Frozen stars and a full moon rising shed a meagre light. His trouser legs flapped in the wind, and melt-water splashed beneath his boots. Fire, in such circumstances, seemed unimaginable, yet in one sodden backpack, wrapped in greased-linen bundles, he found the means and Dagda did the rest.

On a flat stone the small fire blazed brightly, increasing the darkness around it, and Dagda made stew in a retrieved cook-pot with a selection of recovered vegetables, hot and reviving, and scraps of damp bread that filled Roderick's stomach. For that much, at least, Roderick was grateful, and grateful, too, for the massive body against which he leaned that sheltered him from the wind. He was glad the troll had survived. It was something alive beside himself, its body-heat seeping through the woven bark jacket and into him, its great dugs pillowing his head.

Dagda was female, he realised with surprise, a great troll mother as nurturing as any human woman. Yet she had marched with the rest of her kind to attack the dwarven stronghold of Stonehast. It was instinct, he supposed, to protect the lands of her people. And beyond the fire, a pair of blue eyes regarded her, loaded with hate.

Dagda was too short-sighted to notice the sorcerer was alive. Her world was misted and indistinct beyond the limits of her vision, and Roderick was not yet ready to inform her. Trussed as he was, the man could pose no further threat, Roderick decided. And he needed to gain the rock troll's friendship, not revive her anger. Keeping careful watch on the injured Mage, he began to question Dagda.

"What made you believe what the sorcerer said?" he asked.

Dagda sighed deeply.

"Perhaps we wanted to believe it," she confessed. "Elves and dwarfs have long been our enemies and old hatreds do not easily die. Easier to believe they wished us ill than mistrust centuries of troll opinion."

"But why should you think they planned to attack you?"

Dagda sighed again. "Such an alliance it was between elves and dwarfs that drove the giants from Llandor," she replied. "And we trolls are cousins to that race. We have always feared the same may happen to us."

"But what made you think the Grimthane would protect you?"

"That was the offer made and the deal we struck," Dagda said simply. "For delivering you to Asgaroth we rock trolls gained the protection of all the Grimthane's forces, or so we were told."

"An army in exchange for one individual? And you never doubted that the Grimthane would keep his word?"

"The sorcerer claimed to speak as his ambassador, so why should we have doubted?" asked Dagda.

"That's how evil works," muttered Roderick. "It feeds upon our fears and trades in lies, and always has. About those we hate, we're ready to believe whatever we're told. It was the same in my world, too. We divide ourselves up by race or nation, religious conviction or political persuasion, and fear and hate anyone who's not like us. I thought, when I came to Llandor, things would be different. But they aren't. The same fears and hatreds we are prey to on Earth still apply. Trolls hate dwarfs, dwarfs hate goblins..."

"Not all of us," a gruff voice croaked.

Roderick leapt to his feet. He thought, for a moment, it was the sorcerer who had spoken, but the man's eyes were closed again. Then, nearby among the rocks beyond the circle of firelight, the elven cloak that Roderick had draped over Diblin's body twitched and shifted, and the dwarf's bearded face appeared beneath the reflections of flames and darkness.

"I don't hate goblins," growled Diblin.

Roderick laughed. And Dagda, laying aside her enmity, moved ponderously from her seat, picked up the unprotesting dwarf and carried him to the fire. He was bruised and battered and frozen to the marrow, but at least he was alive.

Later, warmed and cradled, fed on scraps of bread and the remains of the stew, the dwarf warrior slept with his head in the troll's lap, oblivious of the indignity. They might even become friends, thought Roderick. It had happened before between Diblin and Umla, centuries of detestation between dwarfs and goblins grudgingly overcome in mutual liking. So why should Diblin and Dagda not put aside their hatred and become friends, too?

"We ought to go," Roderick said sleepily. "If you carry Diblin we can be halfway down the Giant's Stairs by morning. Do you hear me, Dagda?"

The troll's only answer was a quiet snore. And maybe tomorrow would be soon enough to leave, thought Roderick. He was tired, too, and the stars shining brightly in the sky above Llandor promised a fine day for a journey.

When Roderick awoke the first thing he saw were crows perched on the rocks around him, thousands of crows, their black wings sheened with light and their dark beady eyes blinking in the sunrise. Then, in the shadows where the night still lingered, he saw other eyes, round and milky, a horde of grey goblin faces peering round the boulders. Some had bald heads. Some, like Umla, were graced with tufts of hair. All had large pointed ears that pricked in his direction, vicious teeth and sharp two-pronged spears. None of them looked friendly.

"Dagda!" hissed Roderick. "We've got company!"

The troll opened her eyes.

Diblin scrambled from her lap and leapt to his feet.

"Toad-spawn!" growled the dwarf. "Let's get out of here!"

"I think not," a woman said softly.

Roderick turned to look.

Whether she was old or young, he could not tell. Her face was smooth and ageless, her eyes golden as amber, golden as the gown she wore beneath her cloak. And that was black, black as her hair, black as her gaze – twin pupils fixed on his countenance, staring into his mind. She knew what he had done. He had attacked the sorcerer who now sat grim-faced and unbound on a nearby boulder. And she also knew he was not Craig.

Her golden eyes flashed with anger, and her soft voice threatened.

"You will pay for your trickery, boy!"

"Trickery?" muttered the sorcerer.

"This boy is not the one we want, Gerwyn!"

"But he fits your description, Merrigan!"

"His hair, maybe, but not his face! I have seen Craig before, remember? And sources inform me he has entered Irriyan and is out of our reach! This is not Craig, Mage! You have been fooled by an imposter!"

"Another?" murmured Dagda.

"I can explain," Roderick said hurriedly.

"You will explain nothing!" Merrigan said harshly.

She raised her arms to strike – a sorceress, a shape-changer, one who had sold her soul to evil. Roderick thought he would die where he sat. But death was too swift and kind a punishment for Merrigan to impose, and she lowered her arms again.

"Bring him!" she cried to the goblins. "If his life is no use for bargaining, he can serve with his labour! Bring him to Asgaroth! The rock troll, too! And the dwarf who is with him!"

Pulling up their leather hoods, gibbering and snarling and squinting in the early morning sunlight, the goblins emerged from the shadows to surround them. Pronged spears jabbed hard at the back of Dagda's knees, poked Roderick's midriff, and prodded a protesting Diblin into line.

"Now, march!" commanded Merrigan. "And hear this well," she said to Roderick. "It is the dwarf and the troll who will die if ever again you choose to cross me!"

CHAPTER THREE

The unicorns moved like the wind, their hooves barely touching the ground, the landscape a blur of darkness around them. It was a wild exhilarating ride over hills and through valleys, along wooded bridle paths where flashes of coloured lights marked the existence of elven communities. Now and then Carrie caught glimpses of revelry in open glades, heard snatches of music that were instantly gone. The majority of elves were arboreal, Janine informed her, dwellers of the woods and trees. But the strung lights dimmed as the night grew later and the unicorns galloped on.

On and on through the small silent hours before morning, across rainbow streams and silvery rivers, over pasture lands glittering with dew. On through forests where the auras of leaves shone golden and ghostly, and shafts of moonlight slanted through the trees that towered above their heads. And on again, westwards across a vast plain gemmed with shining spots of firefly colours, luminescences of flowers in an ocean of rippling grass.

"Isn't it wonderful!" Carrie cried.

"Magic!" yelled Craig.

"Until it fades!" shouted Gwillym.

"But it will always be Irriyan!" Janine shrilled in reply.

The elves who escorted them laughed at their delight and Garriel, who rode beside Janine, openly applauded her. Carrie thought she would never forget that ride. Almost she became one with the magical milk-white mare who had agreed to carry her, one with the speed and the motion and the power of Shoshuna's muscles. The wind through the unicorn's flying mane dragged at her hair, and the overhead stars were streaks of light in the darkness. Cloaks billowed, black and silver and scarlet around her. Jerrimer and the elf riders sang and Gwillym joined in the chorus, his fine baritone voice being whipped away by the speeding wind.

Then the first hints of dawn gilded Shoshuna's spiralling horn. The sky grew pearly in the east behind them and the miles of grass turned to a sea of gold that lapped against the shores of distant mountains. As the light increased, the night auras faded and the flowers themselves became visible in the grass around them, a swaying tapestry of colour as far as Carrie could see. And on they sped along a road of pale dust that cut across the plain to approach, at sunrise, the elven city of Elandril.

Built where the Trineway entered Irriyan, on a promontory of the Northern Marches overlooking the plain, it appeared at first to Carrie to be a city built of glass. Breathtaking, incredible, shimmering with a myriad prismic colours, the turrets of its buildings soared into the sky, rose and gold, green and blue and lilac, all shining and as translucent as water. She thought the brilliance would vanish with the daylight, dissolve into the air of which it was made, yet it remained as the morning brightened, growing in clarity as the company drew nearer. She saw windows in its walls overlooking the plain, and a paved road zigzagging up the promontory to an arched gateway through which they would enter.

The unicorns quickened their pace, sensing nosebags and stables and the end of their journey. Spray showered from Shoshuna's hooves as she cantered across the river ford at the foot of the promontory, droplets of light cascading through the clear morning air. "Isn't it wonderful?" Carrie said again.

She must have repeated those words a hundred times already during their journey to Elandril. About Irriyan she could think of nothing else to say. It had that effect, Gwillym had informed her, cast a spell on people, beguiled their senses and made them forget. But Carrie could not believe herself beguiled and nor had she forgotten that Roderick had gone with the rock trolls to Mordican, and Kadmon was dead. The unwanted memories flittered through her mind and, briefly, she found herself recalling the land they had left and another, more dangerous journey.

Yet she had only to look around her and the images were banished by the clatter of Shoshuna's hooves as she followed the unicorn riders up the approach road to the city. They had introduced themselves several times during the night, but their names were gone clean from Carrie's head as if she had never known them. Almost, she thought, it was as if nothing could exist beyond the present and her awareness of her own enjoyment, the land around her and the white mare she was riding. She revelled in the sunlight falling warm on her shoulders, the chatter and laughter around her and the sense of companionship. And when she turned to meet Craig's eyes, she suddenly loved him.

"Do you still want to go back to our own world?" she asked him.

"No," he replied. "Not as long as we stay in Irriyan."

"I'm glad about that," said Carrie.

"I didn't know you cared," Craig said teasingly.

"I've always cared," she assured him.

His answering smile reflected the same emotion.

"If we stay in Irriyan we could spend the rest of our lives together," he said. "There's no reason why not, is there?"

"No reason at all," Carrie said happily.

Although it was early, the gates to Elandril stood open, and Jerrimer doubted if they ever closed. The elfin guards who patrolled the battlements were simply there for show, he said. In Irriyan there was nothing to guard against, except an unlikely invasion of trolls from the north. Since the war with the giants over a thousand years ago, when elves, dwarfs and humans had fought together to free themselves from slavery, the elven race had forsworn all forms of combat. Fencing and archery had developed into games and the crossed halberds that barred their entry to the city parted as Gwillym stated their purpose.

Carrie rode beside Craig through an archway of rose-red stone and followed the leading riders along a street that parallelled the city wall. Sunlight, glowing through the semi-translucent stone of which it was built, made coloured shadows on the cobbles.

And the cobbles themselves looked to be gems – agate, amethyst and turquoise, blood-red garnet and the deep glowing blue of lapis lazuli. She pointed them out to Craig, the streets paved with riches, but he was barely interested. It was the architecture of the city that claimed his attention.

The buildings were grand as palaces, soaring skywards, pinnacled and towered and iridescent with light. Flighted steps led up to pillared porticoes. Arched gateways opened into cool courtyards, shady with trees and bright with flowers. And above the streets were verandas and balconies twined with vines and creepers, narrow walkways and slender bridges joining one building to another. Here and there, along winding alleys, she caught glimpses of open squares with pools and fountains, and at the end of a tree-lined avenue was an open-air market where elfin vendors plied their trades.

And tall trees grew in every available space, as if a woodland had somehow merged with the city or else given birth to it. The air was resinous and warm, full of the scents of fruit and spice and freshly baked bread and the soft sounds of ring doves calling, elven voices singing and half-complete snatches of music. Sunlight shining through the leaves made mottled shadows on the walls and streets. The continually shifting colours were strangely hypnotic, and when they turned into Delbeth's courtyard Carrie almost fell from Shoshuna's back, overcome by tiredness.

What happened then remained only as a series of vague impressions: of an elf-woman wearing midnight-blue robes, a clasp of hands, piercing blue eyes, a forgotten greeting; cool rooms and purple shadows; a meal of bread and cheese and fruit, a sunken bath full of warm rose-scented water and Craig's parting kiss; a sunlit balcony, a bed with a white coverlet and blue gauzy curtains surrounding it; a soft voice bidding her sleep.

She awoke sometime later, lay for several moments remembering where she was. The blue gauzy curtains billowed in the breeze from the open window and the room beyond looked dim and shadowy, luminescent with evening. In Delbeth's house she had slept away the day and, downstairs, Craig would be waiting. The elven city of Elandril had yet to be explored.

Hurriedly Carrie rose, and drew back the bed curtains. Someone had taken away her clothes while she slept, but draped over the back of a rattan chair was a lavender-grey gown fashioned from some shimmering gossamer-like fabric. She tried it on and it fitted her perfectly. Then, selecting a ripe peach from a bowl of fruit on a small carved table, she stepped outside onto the balcony to survey the view.

Janine, leaning on the balustrade, turned her head. "I had begun to think you would sleep for ever!" the elf girl said.

Carrie gaped at her. Had they passed in the street she would not have recognised Janine. She was not the same love-struck girl who had left her home at Woodholm to follow Gwillym. She was a woman grown tall and beautiful as Keera, her mother. Her hair, washed clean and loosed from its customary plait, was pale as moonlight, waist-long strands drifting in the breeze. And her eyes, blue as the gown she was wearing, gazed at Carrie in similar surprise.

"You look different," she said.

"So do you," said Carrie.

"It's our clothes, I suppose," said Janine. "We are not used to seeing ourselves in dresses such as these."

Carrie leaned on the balustrade beside her. They were high above the battlements of the city in a tower built of smoky-blue stone. Pale purple wisteria clad its walls and the view was clear for miles across the plain below. She could see the river they had crossed that morning, a herd of unicorns grazing, and wooded hills beyond that were blue and misty in the distance. Peach juice dribbled from Carrie's chin.

"How long have I slept?" she asked.

"Since the day before yesterday," said Janine.

"Two and a half days? You've got to be joking!"

"No," said Janine. "I only woke an hour or so ago, and Craig is still sleeping. Nyssa says Delbeth instructed her to leave us to waken of our own accord."

"Who's Nyssa?" asked Carrie.

"You'll meet her when we go downstairs," said Janine. "She's one of Delbeth's students being prepared for entry to Seers' Keep. Delbeth has been called away to the Western Havens, so Nyssa is here to take care of us. She's hoping to travel with us when we leave."

"Surely we don't have to think about leaving already?" Carrie objected. "We've only just got here, Janine! Wouldn't you like to stay here for good?"

Janine did not answer immediately, but Carrie could feel her desire as strong as her own. And Janine's genetic roots were in this land. She may have been born in the Rillrush Valley but her mother was an elf and had been born in Irriyan. Janine had elven grandparents who were probably still living here, relatives she could visit, places she could stay. But her voice sounded dubious.

"Perhaps if Delbeth were to accept us as students...?"

"I don't mean in this house," said Carrie. "I mean, why don't we stay in Irriyan? We're safe here, all of us, even Craig, safe from the Grimthane's clutches. Surely it makes sense to stay? And you belong here anyway, and so does Jerrimer. We could find somewhere to live, perhaps? Become part of some woodland community? We don't have to have Delbeth's permission for that, do we?"

Janine shook her head.

"No," she admitted. "Except that Delbeth may not see us here."

"How do you mean?" asked Carrie.

Janine's frank blue eyes fixed on her face.

"Delbeth's a seer, remember? She can read our futures. She will know where each of us should be, where our powers lie and how best we can serve the land. The rest of our lives may not be in Irriyan, Carrie."

"Are we bound to heed her?" Carrie asked.

Again Janine hesitated, paused to consider her reply. Below, the shadows of the mountains crept across the plain as the sun sank lower and a flock of white doves fluttered about their roost. In the sky above them a small hawk hunted, a hovering silhouette against the flawless blue sky.

Carrie watched it for a moment, idly musing. Death meant nothing to the elven race. For them it was simply a departure from the Western Havens to the Sunset Isles. Yet something in Irriyan would die that night, caught in the bird's talons. And the hawk reminded her of something. Some buried memory disturbed by its cry slipped through a crack in her mind and rose towards the surface of her consciousness. She recalled Kadmon standing on the Kellsfell and the hawk wheeling above him. He was dead, Craig had said, and the impact suddenly struck her. She felt within her the stirrings of pain and grief, forgotten emotions she preferred not to own and could not bear. She thrust them away and clutched Janine's arm.

"Let's go and explore the city," she urged.

"I wouldn't mind staying if I could persuade Gwillym to stay," the elf girl murmured.

"So let's go and find him," Carrie said hurriedly. "We can talk about it then, when we're all together. And if Gwillym cares about you, Janine, I'm sure he'll agree."

Janine assented and the lavender-grey gown rustled as Carrie followed her down several flights of spiral stairs. Moonstone lanterns set in niches lit the way, their pale light emphasising the marble swirls of blue and purple in the tower walls, deepening Janine's dress to the colour of sapphire and making a silvery sheen on her hair. Evening stars twinkled through the arrow-slit windows.

They emerged at ground level into a sunken courtyard where a great tree towered towards the darkening sky. Opposite, an arched gateway gave entrance to the street, and on three sides steps led up to a covered walkway that shaded the surrounding rooms from rain or sun. Multicoloured lights strung along the ornate overhang reflected in a raised pool of blue–black water. And everywhere Carrie looked there were flowers, spilling from tubs and troughs at the foot of the pillars that supported the roof awning, cascading from baskets hanging from its eaves, massed in window boxes or thrusting upwards between the courtyard stones. The evening air was sweet with their scents and misty with steam that issued from the open door of the bathing room.

Nyssa's smile was warm as she stepped from the house to greet them. She wore a lavender-grey gown similar to Carrie's which clung to her slender form and, in spite of her hair piled on her head which made her look older, she was much of an age with both Carrie and Janine. Her voice tinkled, sweet and clear as water in a fountain.

"So your friend has awakened at last," she said to Janine. "And have you have slept well, Caroline of the other-world?"

"Yes," said Carrie. "And what makes you call me that?"

"Is it not your name and where you come from?" Nyssa asked her.

"I'm usually called Carrie," said Carrie. "And I don't feel I belong to that world any more."

Nyssa nodded her understanding.

"Delbeth will know where you belong," she said lightly. "She has been called away to a departure in the Western Havens but she bade me tell you that her house is yours until she returns. And Craig is at the supper table if you would care to join him."

"Where's Gwillym?" asked Janine.

Nyssa's smile faded.

"Gone with Jerrimer to watch the evening's entertainments," she said wistfully. Then, gazing at something beyond Carrie's shoulder, a frown creased her forehead. "Forgive me for saying this, Carrie, but there is a shadow standing behind you, a kind of darkness. I noticed it with Gwillym, too, and even more so with Craig. It is someone or something from the other-world that follows you, perhaps? Or the shadow of the Fell One from whom you have fled?"

Janine glanced around.

"I don't see anything," she said.

"Maybe you don't have the sight?" suggested Nyssa. "And it's gone now, whatever it was. Seeing only lasts a moment, Delbeth says. But just for a moment I could have sworn—"

In spite of the warmth of the evening, Carrie shivered. She wanted to forget about the Grimthane and the world she came from. And hopefully, if she stayed in Irriyan, she would forget. Again she felt the longing move within her. Whatever happened she *must* stay there, she thought, and so must Craig. He, even more than she, needed to be safe from the Grimthane's clutches. And maybe she sensed, as she and Janine followed Nyssa into the dining room and saw his blue eyes widen in astonished recognition, that only in Irriyan could she love him.

"We've *got* to stay here!" Carrie whispered. "It's imperative, Janine. The Grimthane will be onto us the moment we leave." Blue resolve hardened in the elf girl's eyes. Whatever happened Janine would go along with her, Carrie thought gladly.

Arms linked, Craig, Carrie and Janine wandered up the tree-lined avenue towards the central square where Nyssa had said Gwillym and Jerrimer were likely to be. As it had done before, Elandril overwhelmed Carrie's senses and awed her out of thought. She became one with the sights and sounds and scents and colours, drifting with the music that came from various elegant houses, entranced by glimpses of dancers in splendid ballrooms, soothed by the tree shadows rustling and the sleepy crooning of doves. Buskers and acrobats and street players performed for her entertainment. Evening markets and pavement shops tempted her to buy, although she had neither trade tokens nor goods to barter. As the dwarfs had done, the elves would give, she thought. And a ripe fruit, pressed on her by a peddler who wandered among the crowds, affected her head like strong wine.

Finally the buildings ended, and the paved streets gave way to grass, and the three of them reached the heart of the elven city. There Elandril merged into forest – acres of mighty trees, not tamed and tended as city parks in the world Carrie came from, but ancient and wild as the woods that covered most of Irriyan. Each leaf in the forest canopy above, each blade of grass beneath, were alight with their golden night-time auras. Winding mossy paths led deep into the woods and somehow Carrie knew it was enchanted.

She could feel the forest beckon her. She could lose herself for ever among the shadowy secret haunts of deer and owls, ferns and bracken and bluebells. For a moment she was tempted to do just that, take Craig with her and never return, but there among the crowds of elves on the edge of the forest, sitting beneath a beech tree watching a troupe of fire jugglers perform their routine, were Jerrimer and Gwillym.

Janine threw herself down on the grass beside them.

"Found you at last!" she declared.

"I was not aware we were lost," said Gwillym.

"I certainly have been," said Jerrimer. "Lost from the moment I left Irriyan all those years ago."

"I think we've all been lost," said Craig.

He was right, thought Carrie, as she took her place on the moonlit turf. Now she knew that as long as they stayed in Irriyan they need never run again, nor strive, nor struggle. The land would give them all they required – food and shelter and space to live, the freedom most people in the world Carrie had left dreamed of and never found. They would have to be crazy to leave, she thought, crazy to turn their backs and lose Irriyan's beauty, its magic, its total security – and Craig's smile and the touch of his hand.

"Have you thought about it?" he asked.

"I've been thinking of nothing else," said Carrie.

"Thinking about what?" asked Jerrimer.

"Staying here," said Janine.

"I intend to anyway," said Jerrimer.

"What can anyone possibly want beyond this?" asked Craig.

"Nothing," said Carrie.

"Except a purpose," said Gwillym.

The fire jugglers they were watching bowed and finished their act, were replaced by a group of elves playing flutes and fiddles and a troupe of dancers in shimmering skirts. Their music was as wild as a dwarven shindig but a thousand times sweeter, and the dancers moved with a grace no dwarf or human could muster.

"If we can create somewhere like Woodholm," mused Janine, "then that would be purpose enough."

"So why don't we?" said Craig.

"On the banks of the River Avar," murmured Jerrimer.

"That would be wonderful," said Carrie.

"We could run a ferry service," Jerrimer went on. "Make ourselves a small fleet of coracles. Weave willow baskets and gather fresh-water pearls…"

"Wild fruits and mushrooms too," said Janine.

"A lifetime of sun and water," murmured Jerrimer.

"It sounds idyllic," said Craig.

"Except that we are not belonging in Irriyan," Gwillym objected.

"Who says that?" Craig demanded. "There's no law against settling here, is there? We're not likely to be deported as illegal immigrants, are we?"

"Not if I vouch for you," said Jerrimer.

"Right," said Craig. "That's settled then. We make our home with Jerrimer and ply the river."

"And me and Carrie will keep house," said Janine.

"You are surely not meaning that?" said Gwillym.

"It's what my mother does at Woodholm!" Janine retorted.

Gwillym stared at her.

"The Rillrush Valley is Keera's rightful place!" Gwillym informed her. "It is where she is meant to be, and keeping house is not all she is doing, either! You should be knowing that full well, Janine! She is there for the land! A part of the pattern! Without Keera in the Rillrush Valley the defences of Llandor would weaken and fail! And the same it is with Grandmother Holly on Harrowing Moor, and with Delbeth here in Elandril. Between them they hold the Grimthane at bay! And you, Janine, must take your place among them, Carrie, too, maybe. You cannot be dallying away your lives in Irriyan! You have to go on to Seers' Keep! We all have to!"

"Not me," Jerrimer said obstinately.

"Me neither," said Craig.

"We're none of us bound to," muttered Carrie.

"No," agreed Janine. "We all have a right to choose, Gwillym."

Gwillym shook his head.

"And can you knowingly choose what is wrong instead of what is right?" he questioned. "This life you envision is too easy, see? The trouble with elves, as Grifflin would say, or most of them anyway. They are ceasing to dream and ceasing to wonder of the world beyond the boundaries of their land. And so will you, if you stay. You will be denying what is in you, living a life that is going nowhere and failing to play your part."

"*I* don't have any part to play!" Craig reminded him.

"Maybe none of us do," said Carrie.

"You really believe that?" asked Gwillym. "Even you, Janine?"

Janine chewed her lip as if she wavered.

"None of us knows otherwise," argued Carrie. "Not for sure."

"Quite," said Jerrimer. "And speaking for myself, I have had my fill of wandering. Whatever curiosity prompted me to leave Irriyan in the first place has long ago been sated. I have tried living in Llandor, Gwillym. I have loved Maeve, a human girl, and felt the grief when she died. I have experienced emotions I had never dreamed existed – fear, and pain, and hopelessness, and horror – and I want no more of it. Whatever anyone else decides, I shall be staying here."

"And so will I," Craig said definitely.

"And me," said Carrie.

"It's what I want, too," agreed Janine.

Gwillym shrugged and rose to his feet. The breeze that rustled the leaves of the tree above Carrie's head ruffled his hair and his unkempt beard. Dressed as he was in elven garb – tunic and breeches, thonged sandals and long, flowing cloak – he might have been a mage standing there. There was a power about him, too, a power in his words.

"Stay then," he said, "if that is what you are wanting. But it will bring you no joy to deny the truth of yourselves! I shall be leaving when Delbeth returns. With or without you, I am going on to Seers' Keep!"

"You'd go without me?" Janine asked plaintively.

"If necessary," Gwillym said curtly. "And you should have listened to your mother, Janine. If you want to live the settled life it cannot be with me, see?"

Turning abruptly, he strode away into the

crowded streets of the city. And glancing at Janine, Carrie saw the tears of rejection shimmer in her eyes. The elf girl's sadness touched her, too, in spite of Craig's comforting arm round her shoulder. The music and dancing meant nothing any more. Roderick was gone, Gwillym was leaving, and Kadmon was dead. Irriyan, when Carrie rose to go, was no longer completely perfect.

CHAPTER FOUR

Throughout the following days, as they waited for Delbeth to return, Craig noticed the changed atmosphere. The rift grew wider between Gwillym and Janine. Not only had Gwillym spurned her, refused to stay with her in Irriyan, he had also begun paying attention to Nyssa. It was natural enough, Craig supposed, as Gwillym and Nyssa would be travelling together to Seers' Keep, but Janine did not see it that way. Their easy conversations at mealtimes, their laughter in the quiet of Delbeth's house, seemed to her to be a deliberate affront. Her mood varied between tears and anger and depressed silences, affecting everyone around her except Gwillym, who appeared to be impervious.

Craig began to lose patience. Time spent in Delbeth's house was a strain, and evenings in the city had ceased to be enjoyable. Between them, Janine and Gwillym were spoiling everything, and they were certainly spoiling things between Craig and Carrie. Janine needed her, Carrie claimed. She spent hours upstairs in their adjoining bedrooms, or out on the balcony, trying to comfort and reason with her, and Craig was abandoned, left to his own devices.

Sometimes he could not help feeling resentful. It was the third long hot afternoon he had spent sitting on the courtyard steps waiting for Carrie to join him. Voices drifted from the open window of the study – Gwillym talking and Nyssa giggling, enjoying each other's company as if nothing was amiss. Craig wanted to go in there and shout at them, take Gwillym by the throat and shake him until he saw sense. It was not so much the split with Janine that angered him – that was personal between them and she would get over it given time – it was Gwillym's stiff-necked refusal even to consider staying in Irriyan.

Despite the arguments, Gwillym could not see their point of view. Why resume their journey to Seers' Keep and risk capture by the Grimthane, when they were safer staying where they were? Not only that – everyone except Gwillym wanted to stay. It was the wish of the majority, so why couldn't he simply accept it? And if he was determined to go anyway, then why do his best to make the rest of them feel guilty?

Craig scowled towards the open window. It was emotional blackmail Gwillym was practising and he was using Janine as a lever. If jealousy over Nyssa drove Janine to go with him then probably Carrie would, too, bound by her friendship. And where would that leave Craig?

To himself he was willing to admit it: it was not only Janine who needed Carrie, he did too. She made him mean something at last and he was afraid that if they left the elven land things would be different, that she would begin to despise him as she had before. He remembered their journey through Llandor, his sense of isolation and his despair at being in a world where he did not belong. And Seers' Keep would be the ultimate negation, a place where Craig would be faced with the truth that he already knew: in Llandor he could have no purpose, and all his knowledge gained from years of schooling was worth absolutely nothing.

He had to stay in Irriyan, he decided, and he needed Carrie to stay, too. In which case, he thought, he had better clinch things with Jerrimer quickly, arrange to leave as soon as possible. Whatever pressures were brought to bear, the elf would not be leaving Irriyan again and if Craig could enlist his help to persuade both girls, they could depart in the morning, head for the River Avar and the rest of their lives, regardless of what Gwillym thought.

He rose to his feet, intending to waken Jerrimer from his siesta, but first he headed for the raised pool to quench his thirst. Water within a large stone basin reflected his face. His hair, now grown past his shoulders, was bleached by the sun and beginning to curl, his eyes were as blue as the overhead sky – except that he could see no sky. He glanced up. It was certainly there, a sphere of pale cloudless blue above his head where a bird sailed the spiralling thermals on still wings. Yet in the water round the reflection of his face was nothing but darkness, a darkness so complete it was as if the world in which he was standing no longer existed and the sunlight of Irriyan had been swallowed up by the night.

He felt a moment of fear, touched the surface with his hand, shattered his image, then waited for the same reflection to reform. But instead of himself he saw a woman smiling up at him, a woman with amber eyes and raven-black hair. He knew who she was. He had seen her before mirrored in the river at Deep Dell: Merrigan, sorceress and shape-changer, a servant of the Grimthane. Terror rose up inside him.

"No!" whispered Craig. "It can't be you! Not here!"

But her image remained. And as it had done on that other occasion, her face began to change, her nose becoming hooked and beak-like, strands of her hair spreading outwards like the wings of a monstrous bird. And just now he had seen a bird circling above him.

"No!" screamed Craig.

He glanced skywards again. And with talons outstretched the bird dropped towards him, or so he thought. He tried to shield his face, tried to dodge it, but he moved in the wrong direction. Wings beat at him. Spread claws viciously raked his cheek as the bird swept past him, skimmed the surface of the water and smashed the image he had seen there. Blood came away on his fingers, but he barely noticed. The bird landed lightly on the rim of the pool and he cursed his own stupidity. It was not condor-sized as Merrigan had been. It was just a small hawk come there to drink. Its fierce dark eyes reminded him of someone, but before he could even begin to think about who, the bird took flight again as Gwillym, Nyssa and Jerrimer came running from the house.

"Craig?"

"Are you all right, Craig?"

"What's happened to your face?"

"And what was that shadow?" asked Nyssa.

He had no chance to answer or explain. Carrie and Janine came racing down the stairs of the tower crying his name, and hoofbeats clattered along the street. An elf wearing scarlet regalia and an elf woman in a midnight-blue gown, both vaguely familiar, rode in through the gateway. The unicorns that had carried them snorted and sweated as they dismounted.

"Who called on the dark powers?" the elf woman demanded. Her piercing blue gaze swept over the assembled company and fixed on Craig, seeing the gash in his cheek, the blood on his hand, the fear in him that had barely subsided. "Was it you?" she said.

Craig swallowed nervously and gazed at her in awe. She was tall for an elf, almost as tall as he was, beautiful and slender, with the pointed ears and upward slanting brows of her race, her fair hair elegantly piled upon her head. It was impossible to tell how old she was – no one seemed to show signs of old age in Irriyan. Yet Craig somehow sensed an antiquity about her greater than he had ever known, centuries of time contained within her, a might of wisdom and power.

"Was it you?" she repeated. "Did you use my scrying pool?"

He guessed it was Delbeth confronting him, but he had not done as she claimed.

"I only wanted a drink!" he protested.

"Yet something occurred," Delbeth insisted.

"I thought I saw…"

"Go on," prompted Delbeth. "What did you think you saw?"

"It was just a reflection," said Craig.

"A reflection of whom?" asked Delbeth.

"I'm not sure…"

Craig floundered, not wanting to tell her, and looked around for help. It was as if the whole courtyard was enclosed within a bubble of silence. There was no sound anywhere, no breeze overhead through the leaves of the tree, no sounds from the city beyond. No movement either – the breaths of the unicorns were strangely stilled, and, white-faced in the tower doorway, Janine and Carrie stood motionless, watching him with unseeing eyes. Jerrimer, Gwillym and Nyssa were unmoving, too. It was as if time had stopped and every living thing remained suspended between one moment and the next. Only Craig and Delbeth were untransfixed, although trapped by her eyes and her voice and his own fear, Craig, too, felt incapable of speech or movement.

"You are free to tell me what you will," the elf seer said softly. "They cannot hear what we say. If whoever you saw, or thought you saw, in my scrying pool has the power to breach Irriyan's defences, I need to know."

Craig had to struggle to find an answer, afraid if he mentioned Merrigan's name he would be banished from the elven land. Blood trickled down his cheek.

"It was a bird," he said.

"A bird manifested and attacked you?"

"No," said Craig. "It was a reflection, that's all. But when I looked up it was really there."

"Merrigan!" Delbeth said grimly.

"That's what I thought," said Craig. "But it wasn't the same one I had seen in the pool. It was just a hawk. It obviously wanted a drink, the same as I did, and I got in its way. It caught me with its claws, that's all."

For a moment longer Delbeth's piercing blue gaze held him as if she would rake the truth from his mind. Then she released him, raised her face to stare at a window high up the tower. Following her gaze, Craig saw the same bird perched on the sill beyond the bounds of her spell. Maybe it sensed them watching it, for suddenly it paused in preening its feathers and gave a series of soft mewling cries. Its black predatory eyes looking down on him reminded him of Kadmon, yet in spite of that Craig heaved a sigh of relief. The hawk was witness that his story was true, and elves were supposed to understand the languages of birds and animals.

"Why don't you ask it?" he said.

"Mayhap I have done so already," Delbeth replied. "Its awareness is keener than yours, it seems. Had it not intervened between you and the image in the pool, your injuries might have been worse than they are. You had best come into the house and have them tended to."

He barely heard the sounds of re-awakening – he was conscious only of the memory of Merrigan's face in the water and the memory of Delbeth and her powers of enchantment. Other memories, too, old and unwanted, came surging into his mind: everything he had experienced since he came to Llandor, nightmare images of the Grimthane's minions and his own recurring terror. As he followed Delbeth inside, he realised he was shaking.

"Hold still," Delbeth commanded.

Cool astringent stung his face. Water turned red in the marble basin. And Craig was not safe in Elandril any more. Merrigan had spied him, broken Irriyan's spell. He knew the elven land for what it was – a place of hedonistic beauty, lovely and alluring and never changing, shielded by magic from all that was foul. But for him its defences had failed and sanctuary for him had only been an illusion. There was no place that could shield him from the Grimthane, and no person either. Only he could do that, by creating within himself a core of integrity that would hold no matter what threatened him or whatever fears besieged him.

He winced as the elf seer's fingers probed his wounds, but his thoughts went on. How could he do that? he wondered. How could he be like everyone else in Irriyan and Llandor, cleave to principles he did not believe in and a way of life he basically despised? Wherever he went, in either land, he was faced with the same problem. He had different needs, adhered to the drives and ambitions of a different world. He did not belong here and he never would, and everything he was and all he held dear would either be invalidated or denounced as wrong.

He wished he had never looked in Delbeth's scrying pool, wished he could be enchanted once again and forget. Then he could have stayed in Irriyan and been content, just as he had once planned.

The house echoed with voices, elven and human, talking excitedly. He tried to turn his head in an effort to catch what they said, but Delbeth halted him. One hand held his chin, as the other struck mercilessly at the claw marks on his cheek. Lacerations of pain seared through him, making him yelp and his eyes water.

"They're mostly scratches," Delbeth said. "But one goes deep. And I gather you are leaving in the morning."

"Who told you that?" asked Craig.

"It is what is being discussed."

"It's the first I've heard of it," muttered Craig.

"My hearing is sharper than yours," Delbeth replied. "I hear the whispers as well as what is said aloud. A division in the ranks, is it not? And are you not a party to these plans?"

Craig shrugged. He had just spent half the afternoon dreaming up that same plan and now, it seemed, someone had pre-empted him.

"I thought it was up to you anyway," he said.

"You thought what was up to me?" Delbeth inquired.

"When we leave and where we go," said Craig.

Delbeth paused in tending his wounds. "I'm not your jailer," she said. "Nor am I your pilot. It is not my place to command."

"Then why did you send for us?" Craig asked her.

Again Delbeth paused, considering her answer.

"Mayhap I was curious to meet you," she admitted. "The youth from the other world who set the Grimthane stirring with renewed desire, and the girl who sealed the soul of the Black Mage so firmly to our cause that he would choose to die rather than betray. Yes, I was certainly curious."

"Nyssa said you'd tell us our futures and where we belong."

The elf seer's ice-blue eyes looked down on him, and he sensed her compassion.

"Nyssa was wrong," she said gently. "The future is never fixed, not for anyone. What I may see in my scrying pool is no more than a possibility, or a number of possibilities, some of which I can perhaps warn you against."

"I suppose that's better than nothing," said Craig.

Her eyes sharpened.

"You are asking me to scry for you, Craig?"

Once again the fear rose within him, fear of her power and what she might see. But his need to know where he should go, and what he should do with the rest of his life, was greater.

"Surely we all need help to decide?" he said.

Delbeth raised a quizzical eyebrow.

"Have you not decided already?" she asked. "You will be staying in Irriyan, will you not? You, Carrie and Jerrimer, and Keera's daughter. And if you stay in Irriyan, no other future can apply."

"But is it right to stay in Irriyan?" asked Craig. "I mean, maybe we ought not to? Maybe we ought go on to Seers' Keep with Gwillym and Nyssa? How do we know?"

"You'll know," Delbeth assured him. "What else is life but a series of choices? If your choice is correct then things will flow with you. If it is incorrect then they will go against you until once more you are caught by the current of your own personal destiny and swept away. In the end you will always arrive where you are meant to be."

Craig frowned. A few moments ago she had said the future was not fixed, that it was open to any number of possibilities. Now she seemed to be saying the exact opposite, that his fate was inescapable and whatever he did he could not avoid it.

"So if we're meant to go to Seers' Keep, we'll go there, whether we want to or not. Is that what you're saying? Everything's inevitable?"

"Nothing's inevitable," murmured Delbeth. "As we change ourselves we change our lives and our futures, even our world. And if we have a destiny, Craig, that too depends on us. Now hold still. This is going to hurt, I fear."

Pain wiped Delbeth's words from his mind. Her fingers pinched together the edges of the deep gash... pinched and held... pinched and held... moving slowly along its length and regardless of the agony he suffered. And when she released him the line of hurt continued to throb although his touch told him that his face was healed except for a thin puckered scar that ran from his jaw to his eyebrow. It was the best she could do, Delbeth said. He would be marked for life, it seemed, although maybe it would fade with time.

He was marked for life in more ways than one, Craig thought bitterly, as he re-entered the sunlit courtyard. Too many things had happened to him since he had entered this world, and his head was full of indelible memories. The spell that had cloyed his senses ever since he came to Irriyan was broken. He could see the elven land more truly now and it was not much different from Llandor: dust in the wind and dying flowers, the usual carnage of flies caught in a spider's web, intimations of death and decay wherever he looked. Its perfection had been an illusion and the only magic left was in people – in Carrie, Janine and Jerrimer, sitting where he had been sitting on the steps, their warm smiles as they turned to greet him and the depth of their friendship. Or maybe that was an illusion, too?

"Where's Gwillym and Nyssa?" he asked.

"Packing their bags," said Jerrimer.

"They'll be leaving in the morning," said Carrie.

"With or without us?" asked Craig.

Janine laughed. "We'll be leaving, as well," she said.

"But not with them," said Carrie.

"We'll be heading for the River Avar just as we planned," said Jerrimer.

"And Garriel is coming with us," Janine announced.

"Who's Garriel?" asked Craig.

"The unicorn rider," said Janine. "The one who was here just now, who accompanied Delbeth back from the Western Havens. He was among the group of elves who escorted us to Elandril. He rode beside me, remember?"

Craig shook his head. All elves looked the same to him, and all dwarfs, too, he remembered. The only ones who were different were the ones he knew. And he had no reason to remember Garriel.

"Anyway," Janine went on. "Garriel has been thinking about giving up his position with the unicorn riders for some time. He's had a yen to live a more settled life and this became his opportunity."

"He was brought up beside the River Avar," said Jerrimer.

"A place called Greenlea," Carrie murmured dreamily. "He told us about it – all meadows and willows and runnelling water. It sounds wonderful, Craig."

"He has a sister, too," said Jerrimer.

"Is that significant?" asked Craig.

Jerrimer grinned. "Not to you, I hope."

So Maeve, too, was gone, thought Craig. This land had finally erased even her from the memory of the elf who loved her. Or maybe Jerrimer had simply recovered from his grief at her death and decided it was time to love again? And what else was there to do in Irriyan except eat and drink and couple, dance away the nights and days? The trouble with elves, Grifflin had said. And if they worked at all it was just another pleasure.

"I'm sure you'll like him," said Janine.

"Who?" asked Craig.

"Garriel," said Janine. "We're meeting him this evening at one of the pavement cafés." She raised her face to the sunlight and smiled happily. "And I don't care any more what Gwillym does!" she stated. "I even feel glad he's going with Nyssa."

Craig stared at her with a feeling of shock. From Gwillym to Garriel, Janine had transferred her affections and transferred her dreams. For a moment he could not believe it of her. Janine was not fickle! She was true as her parents, Kern and Keera, loving for a lifetime and belonging together. How could she possibly cease to care about Gwillym? She couldn't, he thought. It was just one more effect of the elven land, her new-found love for Garriel another illusion, an attraction that did not really exist. And was it an illusion between himself and Carrie, too?

He turned cold at the very thought, but the suspicion would not go away. She had made it perfectly clear how little she liked him before they entered Irriyan, and why should that have changed? He and she were still the same people, except that she was enchanted, incapable of knowing him for what he really was or herself either. He glanced at her and found her looking at him anxiously.

"You don't mind?" she said.

"Mind what?" he asked.

"You don't mind if Garriel joins us?"

"Why should I mind?" he replied.

She kissed his cheek.

Craig was not sure whether or not he minded about Garriel joining them, but in any case it was irrelevant. If Delbeth was to be believed, whatever happened next and in the future was not up to him. He could impose his opinions, accept or object, go his own way or go with Carrie, and it would make no difference. They were none of them free to make their own decisions. What he, or they, or anyone did now was all the same to Craig. So he may as well go along with them, he thought, head for the River Avar and hope, for a while at least, to enjoy the game.

CHAPTER FIVE

With Garriel they joined a street party, laughed away the evening and danced away the night. Dawn was showing pink in the east as they returned to Delbeth's house, and the sun had passed its zenith when Carrie awoke. In the adjoining bedroom Janine slept on. Craig and Jerrimer, too, continued to sleep, their doors firmly shut as she crept down the stairs of the tower. What greeted her below was a makeshift meal on the dining table, but there was no sign of Delbeth, nor of Gwillym and Nyssa.

Where the elf seer had gone, Carrie had no clue, but Gwillym and Nyssa had obviously already left for Seers' Keep. She had missed their departure, missed saying goodbye. A part of her felt deeply saddened. She had known Gwillym for a long time now. He had been with them since they first entered Llandor, travelled with them from the time they left Woodholm. He was as dear to her as a brother, as dear as Roderick had been and, as with Roderick, she would probably never see him again.

She sighed, and filled a plate with cheese and bread and fruit. If not for Craig and Janine she would have gone with him, she thought. However much she loved the elven land, she would have gone. But Craig had to stay to avoid the Grimthane, and now that Janine had something going with Garriel she, too, would have no wish to leave. For Craig's safety and Janine's happiness, the loss of Gwillym was the price Carrie would have to pay. Food that should have been delicious tasted like straw, and the fruit was bitter. Or maybe the magic of Irriyan was wearing thin? Gwillym had said it would after a time.

She sighed again and went out into the courtyard. There, too, there was a kind of dullness about things. The flowers wilted in the heat, their colours seeming less exuberant than before, their petals grimed with summer dust. Chipped plant-pots, broken paving stones, faded fascia-boards on the awning and bare wooden doors and window frames gave an overall air of neglect. The whole place needed attention, thought Carrie. And there were bird droppings beneath the tree, dead leaves floating on the surface of the pool.

She leaned on the raised rim and scooped them away, making a small sodden pile at her feet, watching the ripples spread and fade until the dark stillness returned. It was odd, she thought, but the pool reflected nothing, not even the sky or her face. Intently, she stared into its depths. From within, the darkness began to coalesce and an image began to form, a tall hooded figure whose black robes billowed in some unseen wind. Just for a moment Carrie saw him Kadmon with his proud hawk-like nose, his lean face shadowed by his hood, laughter twinkling in his eyes. She saw the movement of his lips and heard him speak her name.

"Carrie!"

His voice had come from somewhere behind her. She spun round, but there was no one in the courtyard apart from herself, and when she turned back to the pool Kadmon's image was gone. She had imagined him, she thought. She *must* have imagined him. He was dead, Craig had told her. He had thrown himself from the Kellsfell. But again from behind her she heard the soft rustle of robes.

For a second time, Carrie spun round, and still she saw no one. Then a movement caught her eye. Perched on the roof of the overhang was a solitary bird, a small hawk outlined against the pale afternoon sky, ruffling its wings. Its dark eyes watched her, reminded her that she had seen a hawk soaring through the skies above the Kellsfell before the bright mists of Irriyan concealed it from her view. Kadmon had been a flesh-sharer, Craig had said. Was it possible he had survived? she wondered. His flesh-and-blood body destroyed in the fall but his soul still alive and contained in the body of a bird?

"Kadmon?" she whispered.

She was never to know if it was he. The hawk screamed and took flight, darted across the rooftop as someone leading a small chestnut pony entered the courtyard. Its hooves clattered on the stones. Its traces jangled, a pair of wicker panniers flanked its sides, and it pulled a primitive sledge partly laden with baggage. Pony and elf halted in the centre of the courtyard and Carrie stared, barely recognising Garriel without his scarlet garb and his gold insignia.

"This is Elvertine," Garriel said of the pony.

She stroked its whiskery nose.

"Nice to meet you, Elvertine," Carrie said solemnly.

"Is everyone ready?" Garriel asked her.

"Ready for what?" asked Carrie. And then she remembered they had planned to leave that morning. "They're not even up!" she said in dismay.

But time seemed not to matter in the elven land. They departed at moonrise after Delbeth returned, the panniers laden with provisions the elf seer gave them. What little else they possessed (nothing but their elven cloaks and a change of clothes) was strapped on the sledge that Elvertine pulled. Their goodbyes echoed round the courtyard and Delbeth, standing on the steps to the tower, raised her hand in a final farewell. Her face was pale with moonlight, her flawless skin stretched tight across the bones of her skull, her eyes invisible and sunk in their shadowy sockets. Briefly, looking back at her, Carrie saw how old she was, a skeletal form bound soon for her own departure to the Sunset Isles and the death that Irriyan denied.

A quick fear filled her. Who would defend the elven land when Delbeth was gone? Who would be wise enough and powerful enough to take her place? It could not be Janine if she stayed in Irriyan and lived her life with Garriel. Janine needed to go to Seers' Keep, needed to learn and grow before she could become as Delbeth or her mother. Suddenly, Carrie realised Janine was doing the wrong thing. They were all doing the wrong thing – hiding from themselves, just as Gwillym had said. But as soon as she blinked the recognition fled and Delbeth looked young and lovely again, an ageless woman who would maybe live for ever.

Of Delbeth and Elandril Carrie took nothing with her but memories and those, she had begun to realise, were not necessarily true. But the beauty of the elven city held as they walked along the street. The sledge rattled over the cobbles, and although the daytime colours of its buildings were dimmed by the frail luminescences of trees and flowers and creepers, it was still magical and alluring.

"Why *are* we leaving?" Carrie asked.

"You'll know when you see Greenlea," Garriel said gaily.

"Everywhere's beautiful in Irriyan," Jerrimer assured her.

"And we can always come back to Elandril," said Janine.

"I wouldn't bank on it," said Craig.

Carrie linked arms with him. "Is something wrong?" she inquired.

"Not with me," he informed her.

"What then?" she questioned.

"I just don't believe it any more," he sighed.

"What?" she asked him.

"Everything," he replied.

"You're surely not regretting what we're doing?"

He shook his head. "Not exactly," he said. "I just can't believe it will happen, that's all."

"But it already is," Carrie insisted. "It's happening right now, Craig. We're going to stay in Irriyan just as we planned."

The city gates released them and the road wound down the promontory to the plain below. No unicorns for this journey, just Elvertine's steady plod as he carried their baggage, and the pace of their own walking. Elves had no use for wheels, Jerrimer replied in answer to Craig's question. The miles of grass, rippling black and silver to the far horizon, would probably take them two or three days to cross.

It was pleasant enough to begin with. They were light-hearted, all of them, full of dreams about the future, and the night was bright and fine, although the air was somewhat chill. Scents born by the wind hinted of autumn, and Craig for a while seemed unaccountably quiet. Carrie could not understand why, but the fact that the wheel was rejected in Irriyan bothered him enormously. It was indicative, he said, of something radically wrong with the whole elven race. His arrogance annoyed her. For a while after that, it was the elves she chose to walk beside, and Craig walked alone some distance behind, sullen and brooding, until he came to his senses and rejoined them.

And wheels were not the only convenience Irriyan lacked. There was no bridge across the river either. Bare-footed, carrying her sandals and hoisting up her grey gossamer skirts, Carrie waded across the ford. The water was icy, flowing down through the hills from the Northern Marches. Her feet turned numb in seconds, and dust on the other side clagged between her toes before she could dry them. Long grass brushed her legs as she picked her way between the tussocks to sit on a patch of close-cropped turf spangled with flower-light and replace her footwear. A herd of unicorns came galloping towards her, ringed her round, their horns honed by the moonlight, their white shapes ghostly in the surrounding dark. She failed to notice what Craig noticed – something hovering over her, black against the stars.

They walked a while longer, then spread their elven cloaks and settled down among the grass for what remained of the night. Small birds chorused as Carrie slept and a hawk rose from its roost on a stunted hawthorn to hunt for prey.

She awoke when the unicorn nuzzled her face. The sun was high, the grass dried of dew, the empty plains stretching away to the far horizon. The unicorn whinnied softly, urging her to be up and moving on. The rest of the herd had wandered away but this one remained – a white mare, snuffling Carrie's hair, drooling and nibbling as if it loved her.

"Shoshuna?" said Carrie.

The unicorn snorted and tossed her head.

"Is it you, Shoshuna?"

She could not tell. But the day was already half done and they had a long way to travel. Laughingly, Carrie shoved the unicorn aside, rose to her feet, ran her hands through her hair, shook the creases from her skirts, and woke the others.

They hitched Elvertine to the sledge, breakfasted

as they walked on cheese and bread, and bilberries gathered from the nearby bushes – and the unicorn followed. She continued to follow throughout the rest of the day, in spite of all their efforts to drive her away. They pitched camp at nightfall, thinking she would leave them while they slept and gallop off to rejoin her companions, but it was she who awoke them soon after sunrise, whinnying and stamping outside the tents that Garriel had brought on the sledge, urging them once again to be moving on.

The morning was sunless. South and east, in the direction they were heading, low clouds misted the hills with a promise of rain. The first rain since they had entered Irriyan, thought Carrie, and it had to happen while they were in the open with no place to shelter. She unpacked their cloaks from the sledge in readiness, although Garriel claimed that with a full day's march in front of them they could be off the plain and spend the night at a farmstead.

"But not with a unicorn in tow," he added.

"Why not?" asked Carrie.

"If she stays with us we are likely to be shunned as outlaws," Jerrimer said. "Be condemned for the worst crime an elf can commit, apart from killing."

"In Irriyan no one can own a unicorn," Garriel explained. "And none but the unicorn riders can remove one from their grazing grounds on the plains of Elandril."

"But you *are* a unicorn rider," Janine reminded him.

"Not any more," said Garriel.

"So what are we going to do about her?" asked Craig.

"I'll take her back where she came from," Garriel sighed.

With Elvertine's halter the elf tried to capture her, but she cantered away beyond his reach. He tried tempting her towards him with soft words and scraps of bread, but she refused to be cajoled. They set out for the hills after that, ignoring her as if she was not with them, but again she followed. Then they split up. Garriel, Janine and the pony headed back towards the city, but the unicorn was not to be fooled. She continued to follow Craig, Carrie and Jerrimer. And when Jerrimer turned back, she followed Craig and Carrie. And finally she followed Carrie alone until she, too, turned back towards Elandril. Only then did the white mare, whom Carrie thought of as Shoshuna, stand her ground, staring after her with puzzled eyes before bending her head to graze as if that had been her intention all along.

It was a whole day wasted. For many miles they retraced their steps before veering south and east in a great half-circle to make for the hills again. The rain caught them by mid-afternoon, a thin drizzle that beaded Elvertine's coat and dripped from his mane and tail, runnelled from their cloaks, soaked the grasses and chilled their feet. They were still on the plain when nightfall came and there was no dry place to camp. Cold and damp, they huddled together in one of the two tents, and shared the inevitable supper of cheese and fruit and bread.

As the wet twilight deepened, Janine talked longingly of Woodholm, of the steaming warmth of the bathing room and the firestones in Keera's kitchen. Jerrimer remembered the vegetable stews Maeve's mother used to make, and evenings spent round the pot-bellied stove in the Boar's Head tavern on the outskirts of Droon. And Craig, in an unthinking moment, recalled the illicit meals of another world – roast beef, pork chops and hamburgers.

"Are you serious?" asked Garriel.

"We used to eat meat where we came from," Carrie confessed.

"In that world they actually raise animals in order to slaughter and devour them," said Janine.

"How disgusting!" said Garriel.

"Worse than goblins," agreed Jerrimer.

"I don't remember you choosing to starve rather than eat eel stew," Craig retorted.

"At least I did not stuff my face with Umla's rabbit," said Jerrimer.

"Who's Umla?" asked Garriel.

"Let's not change the subject," said Janine. "Garriel wants to hear about your world, Craig."

"We're trying to forget it!" Carrie objected.

"Who is?" Craig asked belligerently.

"We used to go there at one time," Garriel mused. "I remember my grandfather telling me, before he left for the Sunset Isles. In the days when the portals stood open between our two worlds, we elves used to go there quite often. Its woods and moors were wild beyond imagining, my grandfather told me. We used to ride the chase while humans slept. And, in those days, it was not unusual for an elf to return with a human lover. But the forests were felled to make way for more and more people, and the moors were put to the plough. Your world grew crowded and dangerous, and one by one, fearing for the security of our own lands, we closed the portals… "

"Who's 'we'?" Craig asked sharply.

"The Seers," said Garriel.

"You mean they actually have control over these gateways?"

"They were never gateways exactly," said Jerrimer. "They were just places where the invisible boundaries between our two worlds wore thin, tears in the fabric of the ether that the Seers repaired. Not many rifts appear nowadays. The Seers have become attuned to the slightest shift."

"It's what Kadmon was telling us about," said

Janine. "The web of power that protects our lands. It's not only there to protect us against the Grimthane but from your world, too."

"So that's what happened!" Craig said bitterly.

"You took us by surprise," said Janine.

"And the Seers repaired the flaming gateway!" said Craig.

"I'm sure it wasn't intentional," Carrie said hastily.

But Craig was in no mood to listen. His fists clenched. His eyes blazed. The scar on his face knotted and twisted, and his voice was harsh with rage. "They repaired it!" he said furiously. "Blocked it before we could find our way back through! Cut off our exit! We could have gone home, all three of us! We could have gone on living our lives! There wasn't any need for us to stay! And I could have been through university by now! I could have been halfway up the ladder, earning a decent salary, and with a place of my own and a car! Instead I'm stuck where I don't want to be!"

"But you did," said Carrie.

"Did what?" snarled Craig.

"You did want to be here. You wanted to stay with me in Irriyan! You said you did!"

"Plying the river," said Jerrimer.

"All of us together just as we agreed," Janine said earnestly.

"You were there when we finalised our plans," said Garriel.

"You can't have changed your mind already," said Carrie. "We haven't even got there, Craig! We haven't even begun!"

She saw his anger fade, replaced by dismay, and she guessed what had happened. He was cold and tired, disenchanted by the weather. In the damp dreary twilight he had temporarily lost sight of the loveliness of the elven land, and too much talk had reminded him of the world they came from and the life he had led there. The old Craig crept through the cracks in his memory – scathing, angry, dissatisfied, full of hate and needing to blame. She reached for his hand, seeking to reassure him.

"It will be all right," she insisted. "You'll enjoy it once we reach Greenlea and settle down. We're safe in Irriyan, Craig, safe for ever. And as long as we love each other there's nothing more we need."

He seemed to believe her, seemed to become reconciled. His mood lightened and he talked with Jerrimer about building a skiff. But later and apart from him, as Carrie lay unsleeping beside Janine, listening to the rain drum on the roof of their tent, she began to wonder if she believed herself.

When she crawled from the tent the next morning into the grey wet light of another day, she saw Shoshuna had rejoined them. It seemed there was nothing they could do but accept her. The blasted animal, as Craig called her, obviously intended to follow wherever they went. Her pale ghost-like presence, shrouded by mist and dewed by the persistent drizzle, dogged their footsteps as they travelled on.

In a land where the seasons mingled and winter seldom came, two days of rain was unusual. The plains turned to bog in places but by evening they were well into the hills, winding along leafy lanes between cow pastures and open commons.

They asked for shelter at a thatched farmstead but the elf wife, seeing the unicorn and not seeing Garriel's insignia, was reluctant to admit them. Inside the house, brightly lit with moonstone lanterns and warmed by firestones glowing in the hearth, the community that lived there were feasting at a long table laden with food. But the only hospitality Garriel gained was a cold supper and use of the haybarn, oats and a byre for the precious unicorn and the weary pony.

Again Carrie lay unsleeping, listening to the fiddle music playing and elven voices singing late into the night. Her own exclusion saddened her and such rejection, she realised, did not bode well for the future. True, they had each other for company, but was it enough? Could they really continue to live in Irriyan if they were to be judged as outcasts by the whole elven race? Deep within she felt a loneliness begin and an overwhelming sense of unbelonging. She wanted to weep for the death of a dream that not long ago had seemed so beautiful.

Tears filled her eyes. They *had* to stay in Irriyan, she thought. For all their sakes they had to stay. And if only Shoshuna would leave them and return to the plains, then everything would be all right again. Determinedly, she rose from her bed in the hay, put on her sodden sandals and crept among her sleeping companions to the adjoining byre.

Pale in the darkness, untamed and untethered, the unicorn turned her head and watched her approach. In the next stall the implacable Elvertine munched his oats, and beyond the open door a gleam of moonlight silvered the unicorn's spiralling horn and the flowing strands of her mane. She nickered a greeting and allowed Carrie to touch her, stroke her velvet coat, her flicking ears, her warm equine nose.

"You know, don't you?" Carrie said. "You know why I'm here."

The white mare snorted, tossed her head and pawed at the straw. Moonlight reflecting in her eyes revealed an intelligence Carrie never doubted was there. And once in Llandor, Carrie had heard a wolf speak and understood its language. Surely now she could speak to Shoshuna and have the unicorn understand *her*.

"You'll ruin everything if you come with us," she explained. "And it's very important that we stay in Irriyan. It's even more important that Craig stays. You have heard about the Grimthane, haven't you, Shoshuna? He wants to take us to Mordican, wants to take Craig. If Craig should fall into his hands then what he knows could maybe destroy the whole of Llandor and Irriyan, too, perhaps. We have to stay here, Shoshuna. But how can we do that if we're outlawed and unhappy? You're wonderful, beautiful, and we'd love to have you with us, but you must go home. You must go back to the plains of Elandril where you belong. Do you understand, Shoshuna?"

The soft dark eyes regarded Carrie, and again the unicorn tossed her head, as if in confirmation. Carrie smiled and patted her and stood aside. The door was open and in a moment Shoshuna would go. Trees beyond the byre moved in the wind, and the loose hay rustled beneath her feet. Mice squeaked and scuttled, their tiny claws scratching on the wooden rafters above Carrie's head. Unless it was a bird? A barn owl, perhaps, its roost disturbed by her presence?

She glanced up, her eyes raking the darkness. And finally she spotted it, its small hunched shape perched on a window ledge up in the apex of the roof, silhouetted by the moonlight. It was not an owl, she thought, more like a hawk. She could feel its dark gaze fixed on her. And then it took flight, wheeling through the doorway with a series of soft mewling cries, and vanished into the night.

Quietly Carrie closed the door, shutting Shoshuna inside. The bird's cries had meaning and she had understood. Its words and a memory of Kadmon's voice echoed through her mind.

"Mayhap, all things happen for a purpose," it had said. "And mayhap, as I do, Shoshuna belongs with you. You would be less than wise to turn away such guardians, Carrie."

CHAPTER SIX

The weather improved. Day after day they travelled on along woodland tracks through the vast forests that lay between them and the River Avar. The warm resinous air hummed with insects, reverberated with bird songs, and open glades were crowded with flowers. By night the woods echoed with a different music – reed pipes, wild strings and elf songs – and the flower-filled glades became dance floors for the elven communities that lived nearby.

Sitting with the others among the long grass at the edge of a glade, or on a fallen log among the surrounding trees, Craig watched and remembered. They were never denied food or shelter, a supply of nuts and fruits, or a bed of bracken in the bole of a hollow tree if it happened to rain, but nor were they made welcome, invited to join the dance, share the feast or enter the elves' woodland halls. The unicorn guaranteed that. The animal herself was revered, greeted with awe and respect wherever she went. But they, who appeared to have stolen her or lured her away from the herd on the plains, were met with a suspicion that bordered on hostility. It was like being condemned without a trial by the whole elven race, and Craig resented it.

After a while, Shoshuna and the general response caused by her presence began to affect them. The joy they had felt at the beginning of their trek was gone. Only Carrie remained untouched by the situation, chattering and laughing and constantly reminding them of all they had planned. And now and then she paused to glance up at the hawk that fluttered through the tree tops, as if to assure herself it was still there, still following them as the unicorn had done ever since they left Elandril.

Craig could never shake off the sensation of being followed. And sometimes on the edges of twilight when the shadows of the forest grew dark and deep, he glimpsed what looked to be a cowled figure standing beneath the trees and heard Carrie whispering. But when he went to investigate there was never anyone there, only the trees themselves, dryad shapes that Carrie claimed to see dancing on moonlit nights.

Irriyan had got to her, Craig decided, affected her mind and made her crazy. He saw her grown wild as the woods through which they walked, her chestnut hair frizzed and unkempt, her lavender-grey gown torn and tattered, and her once pale face tanned by the weather. Her cheerfulness grated and she was totally out of touch with reality. Regardless of how Craig and the others felt, Carrie insisted on befriending the unicorn, fed it handfuls of sweet grass and titbits, doing her darndest to ensure it stayed with them. It was inevitable that someone would snap.

"Leave it alone!" screamed Janine.

"We don't *want* it following us," Garriel said desperately. "And it will never go away if you keep encouraging it!"

"Shoshuna won't leave us anyway," Carrie informed him.

"That's what I'm afraid of," muttered Jerrimer.

"She's spoiling everything!" Janine said bitterly. "Ruining our lives! Can't you see that, Carrie?"

Carrie stared at the elf girl. Through Llandor and Irriyan she and Janine had travelled together, grown as close as sisters with never a cross word between them. But now there was an obstinacy in Carrie's gaze and Janine's cheeks were flushed with anger. They were very near to quarrelling, Craig realised.

"Janine's not asking much," he said curtly.

Her gaze shifted. "So what are *you* asking?" Carrie demanded.

"I wasn't aware that I was asking anything," Craig informed her. "But if we're all going to live together, as you keep telling us, the least you can do is show some consideration towards us!"

Carrie shrugged, and threw down the fragment of bread she had been intending to feed to the unicorn. "It won't make any difference," she prophesied. "Shoshuna will stay with us until she chooses to leave. And the only thing we can do is accept her."

She was probably right, thought Craig. There was nothing any of them could do to rid themselves of the unicorn, yet nor could they accept her. Her white shape haunted them, a thing of ill omen dogging their footsteps and destroying their dreams. They bickered because of her, and continued to be ostracized wherever they went.

The only solution, thought Craig, was to split up. He and Carrie could go it alone, perhaps, and the elves could go to Greenlea, depending on who the unicorn followed. He was still pondering the idea when the forest gave way to open countryside again, the countryside in which Garriel had grown up. Elven homesteads nestled among bluebell copses or were hewn, grassy-roofed, from small knolls in the midst of wild-flower meadows. It was all far too rural for Craig's liking, although the river when they finally reached it somewhat cheered him.

Impossible to tell how wide the Avar was at that particular point. The yellow mists of light that marked the border between Irriyan and Llandor concealed from sight whatever lay on the opposite side. But on the side where Craig was standing the water was deep and clear and fast-flowing, streaming with river weeds and spangled with flowers. Brooklime and crowsfoot and water hawthorn – he heard Janine name them, along with the balsam and flag iris that bloomed on its banks. But of greater interest to him were the shoals of minnows that darted in its depths, and fat rainbow trout lazing in the mottled shade cast by the overhanging willows, although this time his thoughts of grilled fish suppers he kept to himself.

According to Garriel, they were several days' march south of Greenlea and, although they were no more likely to be welcome there than anywhere else, they nevertheless wended their way towards it. Unprotestingly, the patient pony continued to pull the sledge northwards along the river bank and the unicorn continued to follow. The hawk did too, darting and hovering over the open leas. Then, at the twilit end of afternoon when the mists turned pale and chill and began to swirl inland, the tangled banks of a small inlet halted their progress. There they decided to stop for the night, and pitched their tents beneath a colonnade of willows on the edge of the river.

That evening there was no need to beg food from any resident elves, since there was an abundance of wild mushrooms in the fields. Craig, Jerrimer and Garriel gathered fallen wood for a fire, and Janine and Carrie found the mushrooms which they toasted on sticks over the flames. It was the first hot food Craig had eaten since coming to Irriyan. Later, Garriel carved a pipe from a hollow stem, played an accompaniment as Janine and Jerrimer sang, their elven voices sweet and clear as the river runnelling behind them. Warmed by the fire, cushioned in the soft grass with Carrie's head leaning on his shoulder, Craig felt finally content. If this was the kind of life they planned to lead, then he could go along with it, settle and belong in a place such as this.

The next morning it was his turn to capture the pony and hitch him to the sledge. Elvertine had wandered some way away during the night and, slipping the halter over his head, Craig led him back towards the river. Dew had soaked the grass, and pale mist drifted across the meadows. There was no sign of the unicorn. It must have gone, he thought in relief, but then he caught sight of it partly concealed by the tangle of goat willow and elders that grew beside the creek. And someone was with it. Just for an instant, barely discernible among the shadows, he glimpsed a familiar hooded shape, but it dissolved as he stared and in its place stood Carrie. Craig watched as she held out her hand, saw the unicorn respond, allowing her to touch it, run her fingers through its mane, stroke and fondle it.

Raw anger blazed within him as he realised the truth. Carrie could have slipped Elvertine's halter over the unicorn's head days ago! They could have tethered it to a tree, left it for the forest elves to find, and continued their journey without it!

"How long has this been going on for?"

His voice was loud and accusing, and the white mare, alarmed by his tone, kicked up her heels and galloped away, leaving Carrie to face him. And perched in the branches of the goat willow spreading above her, the hawk gazed down on him, its fixed stare dark and disconcerting. But Craig was in no mood to be intimidated by a bird.

"How long?" he repeated.

"Does it matter?" asked Carrie.

"Are you thick or something?" yelled Craig.

"There's no need to get abusive!" said Carrie.

"So flaming well answer my question!"

"Since the night we spent in the haybarn, if you must know."

"All that time?" Craig's anger exploded. "All that time and you could have caught the blasted thing! You treacherous, two-faced...! You knew how we felt about it! All this time you knew and you did nothing! Why, for Christ's sake?"

Janine, Jerrimer and Garriel came running, drawn by the sound of their voices, demanding to know what was going on. Craig told them. All these weeks travelling through the forest being outcast and rejected by every community they came across, and all the emotional anguish they had suffered, need never have happened! Carrie had only to hold out her hand and the unicorn came to her! The outrage he felt was shared by the others, too.

"Is it true?" asked Janine.

"It's true all right!" Craig said harshly.

Tears of hurt wavered in the elf girl's eyes. "How could you do that to us, Carrie?"

"And why?" rasped Jerrimer.

"You knew all along Shoshuna should not have been following!" snapped Garriel. "You knew the problems she caused us. If you could have stopped her, then why didn't you?"

"It wasn't up to me," Carrie said defiantly. "No one can own a unicorn, Garriel. You said that! Where Shoshuna goes is up to her, not us!"

"So you've no intention of doing anything about her even now?" Craig demanded.

"She's a free creature!" Carrie insisted.

"And so are we!" retorted Craig. "If you're going to keep that blasted unicorn, Carrie, then don't expect me to tag along with you!"

"Me neither!" Janine said bitterly.

"And I've no wish to become an outcast for the rest of my life!" said Garriel.

"It's either the unicorn or us!" Jerrimer concluded.

"And while you're about it you can get rid of that flaming hawk, too!" said Craig. "And don't take all day to make up your mind either! We're not waiting!"

He picked up a clod of earth and hurled it into the trees. Then, without waiting to see what the bird would do, he led Elvertine to their camping place, hitched up the sledge already packed with their belongings and set off on a detour round the creek before regaining the river bank. Janine, Garriel and Jerrimer fell in beside him. But, mutinously among the trees, Carrie remained, regardless of their ultimatum.

The four walked on together in angry silence as the sun burned away the morning mists and climbed towards its noonday position in the sky. Now and then one or other of them turned to glance back, although Craig was sure Carrie would follow them after a while. But when they stopped for lunch she was nowhere in sight and nor was the unicorn.

"Do you think we ought to wait for her?" Janine asked worriedly.

"Why on earth should we?" Craig demanded.

"We can't very well leave her on her own, can we?"

"She'll catch up with us eventually," Garriel said confidently.

"Or not," muttered Jerrimer. "As the case may be."

Determinedly, they continued north towards Greenlea. As evening approached, their footsteps slowed and more and more often they paused to look behind them. But the long miles of river bank remained empty and when dusk began to fall there was still no sign of Carrie.

"So what do we do now?" asked Janine.

"I'm not going back for her!" Craig said wrathfully.

"Someone will have to, eventually," muttered Jerrimer.

"We'll give her another hour or so," Garriel decided.

They sat on the grass and waited until the darkness grew complete. Still they waited, until the moon arose, and cold stars blazed overhead. But Carrie did not come.

Craig knew that Carrie had defeated them all and called his bluff. She would know very well that no one, if they had any conscience, would leave her behind. Neither Janine, Garriel, Jerrimer nor Craig himself would abandon her to live alone while they set up house together. She had only to stay where she was and sooner or later they were bound to rejoin her.

Craig rose to his feet.

"I'm going back," he announced. "And when I find her I'm going to wring her blasted neck!"

"She could be hurt," said Janine. "She could have fallen and broken a limb or drowned in the river."

"If she hasn't," said Craig, "she soon will have!"

"I'll come with you," said Janine.

"Surely we don't all have to go?" Garriel sighed.

"Carrie's still my friend!" Janine said fiercely.

"I'll go with Craig," Jerrimer volunteered. "You two go on."

"What's the point in that?" asked Janine. "She's not likely to change her mind, is she? She obviously intends to stay where she is in spite of us, with the unicorn. And we've all been together too long to split up now."

"But wherever we settle we'll need supplies," reasoned Jerrimer.

"Like cooking pans," muttered Craig.

"Salt and spices and oil," said Jerrimer. "Tools and pitch for building a boat. A spade and a hoe. Seeds and rope. A couple of fleeces for extra warmth. A distaff and spindle…"

"All of which can be obtained in Greenlea," said Garriel firmly.

After a brief discussion, Janine finally agreed. She and Garriel would continue northwards, beg what they needed from Garriel's family or trade in the pony, and return as soon as they could. And Craig and Jerrimer would head back downstream, rejoin Carrie and the unicorn, and locate a suitable place to dwell. Garriel unhitched Elvertine, and briefly, amicably, they parted company. But, inwardly fuming and hauling the sledge that contained their luggage, Craig never dreamed as he set out with Jerrimer that their parting might be for ever.

The nights were growing longer now, the days shorter, and the first traces of dawn had barely begun to gild the mists beyond the river when they reached the inlet again. In the half-light they could vaguely make out the unicorn grazing peacefully in the meadow, Carrie, covered by her elven cloak, lying curled in the grass surrounded by flowers, and someone standing among the willow trees nearby. Yet again Craig glimpsed him, a hooded figure clad in long black robes, who dissolved among the shadows and vanished as he stared. A cold shiver travelled up his spine. "Did you see that?" he asked Jerrimer.

The elf's eyes were sharper than his, but Jerrimer had seen no one. It was probably a trick of the light, he said. And exhausted after almost twenty-four hours of walking, Craig was disinclined to argue.

Nor was he about to waken Carrie. The anger he had felt towards her had subsided to a vague annoyance that demanded no immediate expression. Leaving her to sleep, he helped pitch the tent, crawled thankfully inside it and slept.

He was awakened, hours later, by noises nearby of someone crashing through the undergrowth, and emerged bleary-eyed into late afternoon. The river was shaded by the willows and the steepness of its bank, the lowering sun casting eerie shadows on the grass. But no one was standing there, and the crashing noises were coming from the other direction. Craig squinted westwards into the slanting light. The unicorn was quietly grazing on the distant lea and the air was alive with millions of feathery seeds that rose in clouds from the inlet. Branches of clumped elders thrashed as he approached. Carrie, red-faced and sweating and wielding a weathered stick, was hacking her way down the tangled bank towards the water line.

"What on earth are you doing?" Craig shouted.

"There's a boat down here!" she replied.

It was indeed a boat, an old rowing boat waterlogged by recent rain and half sunk in the mud. Jerrimer reclaimed it over the following days, while waiting for Garriel and Janine to return from Greenlea. He baled out the bilge water, cleaned its interior with handfuls of dried grass and polished its oars. It needed painting, the elf declared, but it was still river-worthy. They had themselves a boat to ply the waters of the River Avar, just as they had planned. And that was not all they found.

Many a long hour Craig and Carrie spent hacking down the undergrowth. They uncovered the remains of a jetty buried beneath a mound of brambles, a flight of wooden steps leading upwards through the willowherb and, among the elder thicket at the top, the mud-plastered walls and rooms of what must once have been a dwelling. It was crumbling and derelict and lacking a roof. Green branches grew through the windows, nettles had heaved up the floors and the single chimney was choked with rubbish, but Craig had no doubt it could be made habitable again.

"A boat! A house! Everything we need!" Craig said enthusiastically. "I always knew this was a good place to stop!"

Carrie laughed, flapping at the flies that buzzed around her face. "You're no longer angry then?" she said.

"About what?" asked Craig.

He could imagine the new life so clearly: old trades being relearned, the cottage thatched with rushes, shutters at its windows, a fire oven built from clay bricks mixed with straw. A sewage outflow would be no great problem and they might be able to rig up a pump in the kitchen, tap the stream that flowed underground into the far end of the creek. It was all theirs for the taking, a home by the river with their own private moorings that would be worth a fortune in the world he came from. And there was no mortgage to pay, no need ever to work again once it was all set up. Even their food came free: a constant supply of mushrooms gathered from the fields, nuts and crab apples and cherries in the woods beyond, wild strawberries growing beneath the hedges. And later, he thought, they could have trout roasted in the fire oven, fruit pies and freshly baked bread. Weave willow baskets and trade them for chickens... plant potatoes... cook omelette and chips...

"A life-long holiday!" Craig announced happily. "Back home, most people would give their eye-teeth for this."

Carrie smiled.

"Whatever happened to all your ambitions?" she teased.

"If you can't beat 'em, join 'em," Craig quoted.

"And who needs ambition anyway?" asked Jerrimer.

Craig, Carrie and the elf were sitting together on the jetty, resting from their exertions. Here they were sheltered from the chill wind of the afternoon, and the brown creek water lapped softly around the bows of the dried-out boat. The river looked choppy, its surface whipped into wavelets by the gusting wind which disturbed the hazy barrier of light that concealed Llandor. Now and then they caught glimpses of it – more fields, more willows, a thatched-roofed hamlet beyond and, directly opposite, another wooden jetty.

"We have human neighbours!" Carrie exclaimed.

"No more than half a mile away!" said Craig.

"We're not as isolated as we thought!"

"Convenient," said Craig. "We've no need to leg it all the way to Greenlea. If we need to trade we can trade with them."

"There used to be crossing places at regular intervals all along the River Avar," mused Jerrimer. "And this must have been one of them. I wonder why it was abandoned?"

"Apathy probably," said Craig. "Knowing elves."

"Thanks very much!" said Jerrimer.

"Be honest," said Craig. "Not many elves volunteer to work when they don't have to. You're not exactly a great trading nation, are you?"

"You haven't been to Avaron," said Jerrimer.

"So maybe we can offer a ferry service to Avaron?" said Craig.

"It's days away!" Jerrimer objected.

"Then we'll need to build a paddle steamer," said Craig.

"I thought you had given up on ambition?" said Carrie.

Craig shrugged.

"It's worth filing under future projects, isn't it? Meanwhile, we can begin by re-establishing a direct crossing—"

"The Avar can be treacherous," warned Jerrimer.

"Is that why there's no river traffic?" asked Carrie.

"That's no doubt due to apathy as well," said Craig.

Jerrimer shook his head. "If you don't know the currents..."

"Well, there's only one way to find out," said Craig. He leapt for the boat, swayed and steadied himself, then held out his hand to Carrie. "Coming?" he asked.

She stared at him dubiously. "I'm not sure it's safe," she said.

"I'm damned sure it isn't!" said Jerrimer.

"We won't go far," Craig insisted. "Just a little way out. Far enough to test it, that's all. The water's calm enough on this side and we can always turn back."

"Rather you than me," muttered Jerrimer.

"Oh, come on!" said Craig. "We've got to try it sooner or later. This could be our maiden voyage! You can't miss out on that!"

"I can," said the elf. "If we get caught in an undertow—"

"We'll end up some way downstream," Craig finished cheerfully. "So what? If the worst comes to the worst we can always bale out and swim ashore. Now are you coming, or aren't you?"

"I would prefer to wait until the wind drops," said Jerrimer.

"Coward!" scoffed Craig. "And you're supposed to be a seasoned mariner!"

"Oh, very well."

The boat swayed as Jerrimer joined him, and swayed again as a protesting Carrie took her place in the bows. Fitting the oars in the rowlocks and pushing away from the bank, Craig and the elf began to row. Everything Jerrimer had taught Craig on the river at Droon came flooding back and his strokes were strong and sure, propelling them out of the inlet and into the open water.

There was no danger, no undercurrents. The Avar was as tame as a stream at that particular crossing point, and even the wind had dropped. Further Craig rowed into the haze of light so that the green shores of Irriyan, their camping site among the colonnade of willows, the water meadows where the unicorn grazed and the quiet creek gradually faded from sight. And Craig had forgotten his hatred of the land they approached, forgotten his fear. The human voice that hailed them from the Llandor side was merely an endorsement of the new life he had planned. Turning his head to peer through the mists, he saw a man standing on the end of the jetty, a man in white robes – a monk, perhaps.

"Can you take me across to Irriyan?" he shouted.

"Who's he?" asked Carrie.

"I am Gerwyn, the White Mage!" called the man.

"I thought he was dead!" exclaimed Jerrimer.

"He doesn't look like a ghost to me," said Craig.

"He's been missing for years," said the elf. "I wonder where he's been?"

"I have business with Delbeth!" the White Mage shouted.

"Could be we're about to find out," said Craig.

"No!" Carrie said sharply.

"You mean it might be unwise to question him?"

"I mean leave him where he is and turn the boat round!"

"We can't do that!" argued Craig.

"Please," begged Carrie. "Something's not right. He scares me, Craig!"

"Now you know how I felt about Kadmon," Craig said brutally.

"The White Mage won't hurt us," said Jerrimer.

"And we can't ignore our very first customer!" said Craig.

They bent to their oars and the boat sped towards

him. The wind gusted cold, funnelled from the north down the open water… and in the depths below, among the tangles of green weed, something watched them. A shape, dark and deadly, stirred from its silty bed and began to rise.

CHAPTER SEVEN

The boat nosed into the jetty and Jerrimer extended an oar. The White Mage grasped it, held the craft steady, then stepped aboard. With barely a glance at any of them, he seated himself beside Carrie in the bows. Jerrimer, who was more familiar with handling punts than rowing boats, scrambled towards the stern and used the oar to turn them round and propel them away from the tangle of joists and struts. It was then that Carrie saw something moving in the deep dark water beneath the landing stage, a large sinister shape, streamlined as a shark. A monstrous horse-shaped head, with red blazing eyes and weedy mane, broke the surface. Nostrils huge as blow holes snorted spray, and its lips curled back to expose its fanged incisors.

Frozen with terror Carrie stared at it, remembering the Rillrush Valley and the beast that had attacked them at the ford, the one that had killed the wolf and prevented Roderick from crossing. Quicker than she, Gerwyn the White Mage leapt to his feet and raised the alarm.

"Move!" he howled.

"What?" said Craig.

"Row! Now! For all you are worth!"

"It's a kelpie!" screamed Carrie.

Craig turned his head, compelled to see for himself, and the boat rocked wildly as the creature approached. Jerrimer, still punting them away from the landing stage, swayed wildly and almost lost his balance, then lost it for good as the kelpie snapped at the oar and tossed its head. Too slow to let go, the elf toppled into the river, sank and then surfaced, coughing and spluttering, less than a meter away from the kelpie's snapping jaws.

"Do something!" shrieked Carrie.

The White Mage was already re-seated with his eyes closed and head bent, muttering the words of a spell. Craig lashed out viciously with the one remaining oar, lashed again in a desperate attempt to distract the creature from its quarry. Finally, reaching out and howling at Jerrimer to swim for the shore, he caught the kelpie squarely on the nose. Its eyes blazed brighter, red as balefire, and, curling its lips, the water horse turned towards Craig and snapped again. The second oar was gone, crunched up like matchwood, and gone too by that time was Jerrimer. But the shadows below the landing stage failed to hide him for long and, with a shrill neigh of triumph, the kelpie spotted him and swam in pursuit.

The sights and sounds of that moment would be engraved in Carrie's memory for the rest of her life. Jerrimer's agonised scream as he clung to the struts of the jetty, Craig's despairing cry, bright blood swirling in the water and her own voice calling. "Help us, Kadmon! Help us, Shoshuna!"

By then the boat was already moving fast, caught in an undertow or driven by the wind that came gusting down the river. Faintly, from the opposite bank, Carrie heard the wild whinnying of the unicorn, the mewl of the hawk, but the sounds of them faded behind and were lost in the mists of light that concealed Irriyan. The boat sped on. Hot tears streamed down her cheeks.

"Kadmon, please help us!" she wept.

Gerwyn pulled her onto the seat beside him. "Why do you call on the Black Mage?" he demanded.

"I knew him," sobbed Carrie.

"Then you also know he's dead!" the White Mage said harshly. "As dead as your elf friend and gone beyond the reach of anyone living!"

"But he isn't!" cried Carrie.

"And Jerrimer could still be alive!" howled Craig. "We've got to go back! We've got to try and save him! Turn the boat round!"

"Don't be a fool!" the White Mage said harshly.

Frantically Craig leaned over the side, clawing at the water and trying to row with his hands, until Gerwyn hauled him back. "Sit down!" the White Mage commanded. And when Craig continued to struggle, he clipped him hard around the face and cast him bodily into the bilge. White robes flapped like wings as Gerwyn returned to his seat in the bows, and the wind blew back his hood to expose his facial features. He was sallow-skinned, hollow-cheeked, ginger-browed and ginger-bearded, with thin lips and hooded eyes, icy blue and hard with anger. There was no compassion in his gaze and none in his voice.

"Keep your hands from the water!" he commanded Craig. "Unless you want to get yourself and us killed! The beast will pursue us before long, and there's nothing you can do for the elf! Nothing any of us can do! Not even me!"

"You can cast spells!" sobbed Carrie.

"None that will help!" snapped Gerwyn. "For all his loyalty was suspect, few possess Kadmon's power. My only magic is to harness the wind and the weather, keep us on course and hope we can outrun the devilish thing!"

"We can't just give up!" Carrie protested.

"Who said anything about giving up?" Gerwyn asked roughly. "Self-preservation is the strongest instinct of all! Now keep your heads down, both of you! And keep your voices quiet! The creature is sharp of eye and ear, and your scent in the air could whet its appetite! Get down and stay down, if you value your lives! And allow me to concentrate upon the task ahead!"

Carrie crept aft to where Craig sat. The clout of Gerwyn's hand had left an imprint on his face and he was obviously in shock – cold, shivering, not knowing how to respond. She sat beside him on the bare boards of the boat and held him close. The day had grown sunless, and dusk was falling fast, a chill in the air reminding her of a winter she had long forgotten. But the gunwales sheltered them from the bitter blast of the wind, and she knew that Craig felt the same grief, pain and horror that she did, only maybe more so. Ever since they had met in the Boar's Head tavern in Droon, Jerrimer had travelled with them across Llandor, and Craig had been close to him in a way Carrie had not. But it was she who cried for him. Silently, stifling her sobs, she clung to Craig's unresisting form and wept.

The grey-green banks of Llandor sped past,

willows and alders almost stripped of their leaves. And a host of memories came sweeping into her head. She wept for Roderick, gone into Mordican, his fate unknown; for Gwillym, gone with Nyssa to Seers' Keep; for Janine and Garriel, left behind without even a goodbye; and for Shoshuna the unicorn which she would never see again. But most of all she wept for Kadmon. The magic of Irriyan had actually made her believe he was still alive, his soul born by the hawk, his shade manifesting at twilight among the shadows, his voice murmuring in her mind. It had been an illusion, all of it. Kadmon had died on the Kellsfell, died to protect her, whatever Gerwyn believed. His strength, his power, his love, all was lost to her now. And there was no one left of the original company, no one she could depend on or turn to, except Craig.

Cried-out and empty of emotion, Carrie raised her head. Craig's blue eyes were as bleak and bitter as the day, his face as cold and compassionless as Gerwyn's. That her arms were round him meant nothing to him. He was unaware of her, although he shared his bodily warmth. His thoughts were elsewhere, terrible thoughts, black, brooding, loaded with hatred and anger, and the desire for revenge. Given the means and the opportunity, Carrie realised that Craig would kill – not as Roderick had killed, in defence or self-defence in the heat of the moment –

but ruthlessly, calculatedly, cold-bloodedly, as an act of malice, whoever or whatever or whatever gave him cause.

She bit her lip, searching his face for some trace of the boy she had known, but that Craig was gone. Gone, too, was the youth she had rediscovered in Irriyan, who had helped her hack down the brambles round the creek and shared her dream of spending a lifetime together. He had just been one more illusion, part of the magic of the elven land, as unreal as Delbeth's beauty. Now, with the enchantment ended, another Craig emerged – the one the Grimthane wanted, wounded and dangerous, a threat to the whole land.

Alarmed, Carrie moved away from him. She realised, of course, that he did not have to be this way, but with the hurt caused by Jerrimer's death and Gerwyn's reaction raw and festering inside him, there was little hope Craig would let go of the violent, vengeful self seething within him. For that he needed to return to Irriyan, needed to forgive and forget, sleep and heal and learn to love again.

She turned to the White Mage hunched in the bows, his bleached robes stark in the gathering darkness, his cold blue eyes watching her every movement. She still could not like him, and she sensed the power coiled inside him was greater than he claimed to possess – but neither could she doubt that, having once saved Craig's life by his actions, he would do so again, whatever his motivation.

"We've got to head across the river!" she told him. "We need to get back into Irriyan as soon as possible."

"I'm afraid that's not feasible," Gerwyn replied.

She gestured to Craig. "It's important!" she urged.

She saw the understanding flicker across his face, yet still he shook his head. "If I unravel the spell, slow the boat enough to change direction towards Irriyan, the beast will be upon us," he said.

"It's still following then?"

"The Grimthane does not give up easily, my dear."

"What do you mean?" Carrie asked fearfully.

The Mage's thin lips twisted with the hint of a smile. "Come, come," said Gerwyn. "I recognised you at once – a girl with chestnut hair and a boy with a scar on his face. You are the two who fled with Kadmon across Llandor, the two who escaped Merrigan's army and tricked the rock trolls."

"How do you know about us?" asked Carrie.

"I was told," Gerwyn replied smoothly. "The Grimthane, my dear, was not the only one to surmise you had crossed into the elven land and set watchers along its borders to see whether you left. Fearing just such an ambush as we have encountered, I was sent by the Seers to escort you safely. And providential it was that I arrived when I did."

Carrie stared at him. She had distrusted him even before she met him, although she could not have said why, but now she knew he lied. Craig had had no scar on his face when they left Llandor and, according to Jerrimer, Gerwyn had been missing from Seers' Keep for years so there was no way he could have learned of it from them. His being here was nothing to do with providence and nothing to do with the Seers either. He was there for another more devious reason. They had to get away from him, she thought, now, while they still could – dive overboard and swim for the shore, perhaps? And if Gerwyn had lied about some things, perhaps he had lied about others too? Maybe the kelpie was not following them at all?

Casually, so as not to arouse his suspicions, Carrie shifted to the side of the boat and raised her head cautiously above the gunwales. The wind struck her face, dragged at her hair, and a white wake streamed behind them. Nearby, the banks of Llandor passed in a rush of darkness but, westwards through the mists that hid Irriyan from her sight, fading daylight reflected on the water, grey and glimmering.

She was unable to be sure. There could be a dark shape swimming behind them, or it could be a reflection of the boat itself, a shadow in the swell. She leaned out further, searching for the gleams of red that were the creature's eyes. And the boat rocked violently, buffeted by a sudden squall of wind. Cold spray drenched her, soaked her dress and hair, and her heart hammered in fright. Gerwyn was trying to pitch her overboard, she thought. Her knuckles whitened as she clung to the sides before lowering herself back to the safety of the bilge. Wet and shivering, she turned to face him.

"Satisfied?" he asked her. And she thought, when he moved, that he was about to strike her, but instead he took off his white outer robe and hurled it towards her. "You had best put that on before you freeze!" he said curtly.

Shamefaced, Carrie wrapped herself in the warm woollen folds of the cloak and pulled up the hood. Maybe he was there to help them after all, she thought.

"Where are you taking us?" she asked.

"Where do you think?" he said crossly.

"Seers' Keep?" she said hopefully.

"As instructed," Gerwyn confirmed.

A wave of relief flooded through her, and Craig raised his head, roused from his torpor.

"Over my dead body!" he said wrathfully.

There were a few seconds of profound silence, a pause where no one moved or spoke, where the whine of the night wind and the rush of the river were almost inaudible. Impossible to see, in the surrounding darkness, the expression on Gerwyn's face, but he was obviously taken aback by the vehemence of Craig's refusal, and so, for a moment, was Carrie.

Then she remembered their journey through Llandor and Craig's detestation of the world in which he found himself. She had never really considered how he must have been feeling, trapped in a place where he did not want to be, where everything he believed in and all he valued was meaningless. And it was never Craig himself they had tried to save from the Grimthane's clutches, only the knowledge in his head – physics, chemistry, electronics and practical technology – everything he had learned at school about the achievements of his own world that could be applied to destroy this one. In Llandor, Craig was a danger that would have to be de-activated or contained as long as he remained there, and he knew it. He must be as afraid of the Seers as he was of the Grimthane, thought Carrie.

Curiously intent, the White Mage leaned forward.

"I take it you have some objection to our destination?"

"Darned right I have!" said Craig.

"I'm sure it won't be as bad as you fear," Carrie

assured him. She reached for his hand but he snatched it away.

"It's all right for you!" he said bitterly. "You've got no idea what it's like, and nothing to lose! But I'm not going to give up on myself and scrap everything I've learned, ascribe to a set of neolithic values and a policy of total non-progression just because the Seers ask me to!"

"They mightn't ask anything of you," said Carrie.

"Use your loaf!" Craig said scornfully. "That was the purpose of taking me to Seers' Keep in the first place! And if I don't go along with them, what will they do with me? I'll be incarcerated, won't I? For the rest of my life!"

"Seers' Keep is a very beautiful island," murmured Gerwyn. "As beautiful and magical as Irriyan. Once there, it will cast its spell upon you, Craig. You will surrender to Merganna's enchantment and you will be quite happy to spend the rest of your life there. I can assure you, you will no more wish to leave it than you wished to leave the elven land."

Appalled, Carrie stared at the White Mage. It was the worst thing he could have said. At a stroke he had stripped Craig of his freedom and his right to choose, offering instead a lifetime of mindless enchantment. Any lingering desire Craig might have had to return to Irriyan, and any hope of persuading him to go to Seers' Keep, was totally destroyed. And the loathing that had simmered in his mind ever since he came to Llandor exploded once again.

"So that's it!" Craig said furiously. "That's how the Seers work! Blasted brainwashing! I'll be turned into the same kind of unresisting zombie I was in Irriyan!"

"But you weren't!" Carrie said plaintively.

"Wasn't I?" said Craig. "The way I see it, that's exactly what I was! I always sensed there was something wrong with the place!" He turned to the Mage. "And you expect me to go with you?" he asked Gerwyn. "Voluntarily? Knowing what I do? No way!"

"We'll talk about it in the morning," Gerwyn said crisply.

"You'll put us ashore in the morning!" Craig commanded.

"In Irriyan?" asked Gerwyn.

"Anywhere but!" Craig retorted.

"As you wish," the White Mage complied.

"And you'd better mean it!" threatened Craig.

Gerwyn's face in the darkness was barely discernible, but Carrie thought she saw him smile, and the thought troubled her. Everything about Gerwyn troubled her – his words, his duplicity, the power he claimed not to possess, and her own helplessness in the face of him.

He was not like Kadmon, she thought, challenging her, encouraging her, until almost she had felt at one with him. Slowly and insidiously, Gerwyn had diminished her, undermined her, despoiled her memories and demolished her dreams. All Kadmon had believed of her, and all she had once begun to believe of herself, no longer seemed possible. She had lost faith in herself and lost her sense of purpose. Adrift on the dark waters of the River Avar, with the White Mage watching over her, Carrie no longer knew who she was.

For an illusion of love she had bound herself to Craig, obliged herself to go with him wherever he went, wherever the White Mage decided. And where was that? she wondered. If Gerwyn was not allied with Seers' Keep then he must be a servant of the Grimthane, and it was to Mordican, to Asgaroth that he intended to take them. Terrified, she looked to where he was sitting, a pale shape in the bows, his head bent to his chest as if he slept. She shook Craig's shoulder, relayed her suspicions, her voice almost unheard above the wail of the wind and the hiss of the water. And maybe Craig had not heard, for he made no reply.

"Did you hear what I said?" she asked.

"You could be paranoid," he muttered.

"You're willing to trust him?" she demanded.

"Not entirely," he admitted.

"Then we have to get away from him!" Carrie said urgently.

"That's what I aim to do," Craig confirmed.

"We'll swim for it," Carrie decided.

"Good thinking," said Craig. "And the first one in the river ends up meat for the kelpie! Any more bright suggestions?"

"I'm not quite stupid!" Carrie said stiffly. "In case you've forgotten, kelpies only live in freshwater streams, and the Avar flows into the sea, remember? By the time we reach the estuary it will have stopped following us."

"OK," said Craig. "Supposing Gerwyn's dozy enough to let us slip overboard and reach the shore, then what?"

"We could make our way to Avaron," said Carrie.

"I'm *not* going back into Irriyan!" Craig said angrily.

"Llandor then," said Carrie.

"And the whole flaming issue starts again!"

Carrie sighed. There was too much resistance inside him, too much antipathy. She could see things clearly now – women like Delbeth and Keera and Grandmother Holly would never imprison anyone. The Seers meant Craig no harm, and Seers' Keep was the only place he could go, the only true haven – but she could never convince him of that. He had to choose it for himself, of his own free will, knowing it to be right.

"Where else is there?" she asked him.

"You tell me!" he said bitterly.

"I could tell you," Gerwyn said softly.

Carrie's heart sank. The White Mage had not been sleeping at all, and, for all the noise of the night, he had overheard their conversation. He knew now what Carrie thought of him and would foil any attempt to escape. And although Craig, too, was disinclined to trust him, he had not entirely believed Carrie either. Cynical about both of them, his only choice was to test the White Mage.

"Go on," he challenged.

Gerwyn chuckled. "There is *one* place in this world where you can escape from the Seers," Gerwyn informed him. "One place where you would be welcomed with open arms and feted as a king. I am surprised you have not thought of it yourself."

"Mordican," Carrie said dully.

"And stuff you!" howled Craig.

He lunged to his feet, as if he intended to attack, but he had no chance. The White Mage raised his hand and a bolt of red light struck Craig in the chest, hurling him backwards over the seat so that he fell with a thud against the stern of the boat. Heedless of what Gerwyn might do to her, Carrie scrambled over the seat to where Craig was lying, felt in the darkness for the position of his legs, his back, his neck. Nothing seemed broken but he moaned when she touched his head, and her fingers came from his temple sticky with blood.

"He's hurt!" she said angrily. "Did you have to do that?"

"I'll do whatever I must," the White Mage retorted.

"And so will I!" Carrie replied.

His laughter mocked her. He knew as well as she did there was little she could do. Taking off the white woollen cloak, she wrapped it round Craig's inert body, staunched the blood-flow with a torn scrap of her dress, and sat sleepless beside him waiting for morning. Unseen in the darkness on either side of the river, the lands swept past her, the lands she had travelled through and grown to love. She did not understand the power that protected Llandor and Irriyan, but if she and Craig were ever to reach the safety of Seer's Keep then they were in need of that protection. Wind, water, soil and stone the birds of the air, the fish in the river, the beasts of the land – all that lived and moved and dwelled in that night Carrie reached out to with her mind and silently called to her aid. But nothing came. Nothing wrested control away from the White Mage, and eventually she slept.

It was light when she awoke. Thick mist

shrouded the Avar, concealing even the nearby bank, and droplets of moisture dewed Gerwyn's beard. The wind had eased, although the water seemed choppy as if they were no longer on the river at all, but had reached the open sea. The air tasted of salt, and somewhere in the distance she heard the eerie screaming of gulls.

Desperately, she turned to Craig, and her relief at finding him sitting upright and not lying unconscious was lost in the realisation that they had probably left it too late to swim ashore. And he himself must have realised that. Sullen and brooding, he stared at the sea-mists and the grey–green ocean, and in his eyes she found no trace of hope, just a dull acceptance that wherever he went, wherever Gerwyn took him in this world that was not his own, he could never win. Even his anger was gone. Unresisting and unprotesting, while Carrie slept, Craig had surrendered to a power that was greater than he was and given up the fight.

Now Carrie was truly alone against the power of White Mage. Clenching her fists, she turned to face him. His pale eyes watched her, blue and cold, and she saw him smile. He thought she was helpless, a feeble ineffectual girl, her only weapon her defiance. But she had stood alone before, against Merrigan's army of crows and against Kadmon, who was greater than he. If she could take on the Black Mage possessed by the flesh-sharer, she could take on Gerwyn, too, and she was not alone. She had the power of Irriyan and the power of Llandor to aid her, the magic of the Seers and the sea and the crying of gulls. And the smile on the face of the White Mage faded when Carrie raised her hands.

CHAPTER EIGHT

Craig's only instinct, since the White Mage had felled him, was to sit down, shut up and hope to survive, but Carrie took the opposite tack. With clenched fists she rose to face him. Then, as Gerwyn continued to smile, she raised her hands. There was a power about her that Craig had not realised she possessed, a power in her voice. The White Mage cringed from her curse. His face grew ashen and a hint of fear flickered in his eyes, but then he rallied. His countenance hardened, and his apprehension fled in a blaze of ice-blue anger as he leapt to his feet. And still Carrie cursed him, damned him for his treachery and calmly claimed for herself the control of the elements he believed to be his.

"The land knows you, Gerwyn! There is nothing you can do against it! And nothing you can do against me!" she declared.

She was mad, thought Craig, stark raving bonkers! She had no access to magic, and she was deluding herself if she thought she had! She was just a would-be hairdresser from another world, not as dim as Roderick had been but certainly not clever enough to take on a practising sorcerer. And if Gerwyn retaliated they were both doomed to a dunking in the icy sea.

"For Christ's sake, lay off, Carrie!"

"Keep out of it!" she warned him.

"You don't know what you're saying!"

"I know exactly what I'm saying!" she retorted.

Craig hated her like this, crushing and obnoxious. She was asking for it, he thought, asking for whatever Gerwyn hurled at her. But why should he have to suffer for her overbearing stupidity? He yanked at her dress to make her sit down – and something crackled. Static electricity charged the thin elven fabric, making his fingers tingle and forcing him to release his hold. Waves splashed gently against the bows of the boat, the sea-mists swirled and drifted, and unseen gulls screamed overhead. Any moment now Gerwyn would blast them both, thought Craig. But, incredibly, the White Mage waited.

"Put us ashore!" Carrie commanded.

Gerwyn's eyes flashed dangerously.

"What will you do if I refuse?" he rasped.

"There's nothing she *can* do!" Craig said quickly.

"Just stay out of it!" Carrie repeated.

"Come!" snarled Gerwyn. "Let us see what you are made of, girl! Come, do your worst!"

"No!" howled Craig.

The ocean heaved and a great wave rose, a green wall of water bearing down on them and threatening to swamp them, conjured by Gerwyn's raised hand. There was no hope Carrie could counter it. Screaming at them both to stop, Craig clung to the gunwales as the boat veered and spun. Then, a white luminescence pulsed at the corners of his vision where Carrie was standing. Frail lightnings issued from her fingertips, and a whirlwind called out of nowhere split the crest into mighty fountains of spume. Salt spray showered through the air, stung Craig's eyes, soaked his clothes and hair, and dripped from Gerwyn's beard. Water-spouts danced upon the surface of the sea.

Carrie had succeeded, had turned Gerwyn's power against him – or so Craig thought until his reason denied it. Whatever had happened could not have been her doing, and he must have imagined what he had seen. He watched as the water-spouts died and the mists swirled and parted, dispersing like smoke to let through a frail gleam of sun. Just for a moment he glimpsed distant cliffs and tall ships sailing in a clear blue bay, and another one not far away from them, a three-masted clipper riding at anchor with sailors lowering a long-boat over its side. Knowing they must have been spotted, Craig scrambled to his feet, waved his arms and shouted.

"Over here! We're over here! Help us! Help us!"

Distracted by the sound of his voice, Carrie glanced round.

"Sit down!" she snapped.

"There's a boat!" Craig told her.

She turned to look, but by then Gerwyn had regained control. The horizon tilted, and the blue-green swell began to gather, and the next great wave came sweeping towards them. If Carrie had countered it before, she had no chance this time. Its crest towered above the boat, curled on itself and began to topple.

Her scream was drowned by the roar of the sea as Craig lurched towards her, but a weight of water came crashing down on him, swept him from his feet before he could reach her. He would have gone overboard with her if Gerwyn had not caught him, hauled at his clothes as the sea sucked and withdrew. Coughing and spluttering, drenched to the skin, Craig landed on his backside in the bilge. Salt water puddled around him as the craft righted itself.

"Next time, try heeding her advice," the White

Mage advised him.

But there might never be a next time, for Carrie was gone.

Gripping the sides of the boat and desperately howling her name, Craig searched for a sight of her among the troughs and swells of the surrounding ocean. The drifting mist obscured his view, but terror sharpened his senses. He saw in the distance a pale arm flailing, and heard among the screams of gulls her answering cry. Rounding on the White Mage, Craig forgot about diplomacy.

"She's over there!" he said angrily. "Shift yourself, Gerwyn! We're going to pick her up!"

"Is that an order?" the White Mage said softly.

"Yes!" said Craig. "It *is* a flaming order! You control this boat, so move it! Or do I go over the side with her?"

"That," retorted Gerwyn, "is entirely up to you."

"Is it?" Craig said quietly. "The Grimthane wants me alive, remember? If you let anything happen to me, you won't exactly be flavour of the month, will you?"

"That's the girl talking!" snapped Gerwyn. "The suppositions are hers, not yours! I bear the trust of Seers' Keep and have nothing to do with the Grimthane!"

"So prove it!" Craig demanded. "Turn this boat round and pick Carrie up!"

"Very well." The White Mage shrugged, spread his hands to calm the pitching sea. Once again the mists began to clear, and they saw that they had no need to rescue Carrie. The long-boat had already reached her. Vague shapes of sailors were hauling her aboard as others bent their backs to the oars. Craig's ordeal was almost over. The craft came skimming towards him, and a coiled rope, hurled around the prow, tightened and knotted and took the boat in tow, in spite of Gerwyn's protests. Crouched in the bilge, soaked and shivering, Craig heaved a sigh of relief as the sailors ferried him to safety aboard the waiting clipper.

White sails loomed through the clearing mist, billowing in the breeze from across the bay. High wooden bulwarks towered over him, and her name, *Sea Sprite*, was painted on the curve of her prow. Rope ladders dangled precariously over the sides.

Carrie was the first to climb, with water dripping from her hair and her wet gown clinging. Gerwyn went next, scrambling across the long-boat, his white woollen robes heavy and sodden. Then it was Craig's turn. He had barely noticed his rescuers until that moment but, clutching the hand held out to steady him, he suddenly realised they were not human.

The shock struck him. They were orcs, he guessed, the sea-trolls Gwillym had mentioned and Jerrimer had sailed with. Taller than he was and several times his bulk, hunched and grotesque, with bald massive heads on thickset necks, they ringed him round. Pale fishy eyes from grey dolphin-like faces peered down on him. They were all dressed alike in knitted navy-blue sweaters and sealskin breeches, but their extremities were bare – great flippered hands and feet with blue–black webs between their splayed fingers and toes.

Hastily, repulsed by their appearance, Craig released his hold on the supporting arm and backed towards the nearest ladder, swayed with the movement of the sea and almost fell. The immense grins widened, and unlike most species that inhabited this world, orcs were not vegetarians. Each grinning mouth exposed a set of razor-sharp teeth, similar to goblins' teeth but many times larger. They could crunch him up and consume him in seconds, he thought in alarm. But their deep bass voices were surprisingly gentle.

"Are you all right, lad?" one of them inquired.

"Not found your sea-legs yet?" asked another.

"If you want I can carry you aloft," a third one offered.

Craig shivered, and swallowed his fear. The idea of being touched by any one of them made his flesh creep, although he was already aware they were neither cold nor slimy, but as warm-blooded as he. Spurning their offers of assistance, assuring them he could manage, Craig gripped the rope ladder, scaled the clipper's side in Gerwyn's wake, clambered over the bulwarks and dropped onto the main deck.

Up there the wind was freezing, cutting untempered across the open bay, and the brightness dazzled him. It was all sky and sunlight, sparkling water and vast horizons. And there were orcs everywhere, coiling ropes, setting sails, hauling up the long-boat, winding in the anchor chain and clambering about the rigging. But one in particular caught his attention – a large uniformed orc, obviously the ship's captain, who was standing on the stairs to the poop deck mediating in yet another confrontation between Gerwyn and Carrie.

"We need to go to Seers' Keep!" said Carrie.

"And I have business with the elf seer!" Gerwyn argued. "Business that concerns this girl and the boy, too. I demand you take us back to Avaron at once, Captain Grinnipik!"

"I cannot re-enter the harbour against both wind and tide!" Captain Grinnipik retorted.

"You can with my assistance," Gerwyn assured him.

The orc captain shook his massive head.

"My crew is a superstitious bunch," he said darkly. "And so, too, am I. I will have no sorcery practised aboard my ship! If you are determined to return to port I can spare two of my crew to row you there in one of the long-boats. But the girl stays here. I will put her ashore at Seers' Keep in accordance with her wishes."

"Craig, too?" asked Carrie.

"The boy, too," confirmed Captain Grinnipik.

Craig felt stung. Carrie knew damned well he did not want to go to Seers' Keep and she had no right to make that kind of decision on his behalf! Angrily, shivering in the sea-wind in his soaked elven clothes, he made his way towards them. Astern, the city of Avaron shimmered in the distance through a haze of light. But he was not going there either, he decided, and certainly not with the White Mage. He would go his own way from now on, appeal to the captain, to the orc's sense of justice that had already been displayed. With a little luck and a change of identity, he need never meet Carrie or Gerwyn again.

"I want to go where your ship is heading," he told the captain.

"To Kellshaven?" questioned the orc.

"Yes," said Craig. "And I'm willing to work my passage."

"But we're going to Seers' Keep!" Carrie protested.

"Speak for yourself!" Craig retorted.

The White Mage smiled sardonically.

And the orc rested a reassuring hand on Craig's shoulder.

"We'll talk about it later," Captain Grinnipik declared. "Now take yourself below, lad, and ask my wife to supply you with dry clothes and hot vittles. And you go with him," he said to Carrie. "Is it your wish I should lower a long boat?" he inquired of Gerwyn.

The White Mage shrugged.

"Small difference," he said, "between Delbeth the elf seer and Merganna the Enchantress. To spare you the delay I, too, will go ashore at Seers' Keep, Captain Grinnipik."

"As you wish," Captain Grinnipik replied. His bass voice rose. "Up the main sail, Bosun! Take her out, helmsman! Full speed along the western seaboard, men!"

The sails filled and the clipper moved seawards as Craig headed down the stairs to the mess deck. Portholes let in a gloomy light, and countless hammocks were strung between the ship's timbers, sea-chests stowed along its sides. There was a galley at the far end with trestle tables nailed to the floor, and a figure stirring a cauldron on a great pot-bellied stove. The scent of hot fish stew, spicy and fragrant, filled the air, reminding Craig that he was not only wet and cold but also ravenously hungry.

Behind him, Carrie was still yammering about the need to go to Seers' Keep. "You've got to listen!" she insisted. "It's the only place we can go where you'll be safe! There isn't anywhere else!"

"Give it a rest!" Craig said wearily.

"Why can't you see?" asked Carrie.

But Craig did not want to see. The figure at the cauldron turned her head at the sound of their voices.

"Are you Mrs Grinnipik?" he asked.

His initial prejudice against orcs, already modified by his encounter with the ship's captain, was erased entirely by Mrs Grinnipik. Garrulous and kindly in her voluminous knitted skirts and multicoloured shawl, she proceeded to mother both him and Carrie. Overwhelmed by her massive bulk, and unable to get a word in edgeways, they were stripped of their clothes. The frail elven cloth, torn by their trek through the forests of Irriyan and spoiled by the sea, would do for dishrags, Mrs Grinnipik declared, and there was nowt like a hot bath for restoring the circulation. Heedless of their embarrassment, she ushered them into a vast tub of steaming water, soaped their faces, lathered their hair and scrubbed their bodies clean.

Nothing distracted her either. With a brief nod of her head and a wave of dismissal to the sailor who brought her a message, the orc wife continued her ministrations – searched their heads for lice, their limbs for signs of rickets or scabies, towelled them dry and tended their bruises with strong-smelling tincture. Finally, wrapping them in rough woollen blankets to cover their nakedness, Mrs Grinnipik set them side by side on a coil of rope near the stove and attended to their stomachs. She found bread and cheese and fruit for Carrie, and filled a bowl for Craig with a liberal helping of fish stew.

"Now you bide here a while, my little drowned lambs," Mrs Grinnipik advised. "More's there to eat in the stewpot and the galley if you are needing it. I must away on Grinnipik's bidding and house this mage who's come aboard. Gerwyn the White and in no pleasant temper by all accounts. Such company we could have done without! And I've another poorly young thing to attend to as well, sick from the sea before we left harbour and green as a gherkin. I'll have you both attired as soon as can be – a pair of Grinnipik's breeks, perhaps, and one of my skirts? And I'll find you a berth, too. I shan't be long."

With an armful of sheets taken from a sea-chest, her flippered feet slapping on the decking and her bulk dissolving into the distant gloom, the orc wife waddled away, leaving Craig and Carrie alone together. The stove sang softly and the cauldron bubbled, and the ship rolled gently as the waves slapped against its sides. They were safe at last, for the duration of the voyage, out on the open ocean and under the protection of Captain and Mrs Grinnipik where even the White Mage could pose no threat. Not long ago they would have loved in their relief, thought Craig, but now it seemed that they had nothing to say to each other. The silence grated and, refilling his dish with stew, he could sense Carrie's disapproval. Her long chestnut hair had dried to a frizz and her grey eyes brooded. But he was not the only one at fault. "That was a damn fool thing to do!" he told her.

"What was?" she asked.

"Taking on Gerwyn!" said Craig.

Carrie stared pointedly at his plate.

"I don't know how you can eat that!" she said.

"Easy," said Craig. "And don't change the subject either! You could have got us both killed!"

"But I didn't!" said Carrie. "I got us here instead! And why eat fish, Craig? You're not an orc!"

"Nor are you a blasted sorceress!"

"I'm not saying I am!" she retorted. "But maybe I could be. Maybe I could become a seer and you could become a mage. Something happened back there, Craig. That web of power that Kadmon told us about that criss-crosses Llandor – just for a moment I channelled it. And it's there for everyone – for anyone who needs it and allows the Seers to teach them."

"So that's why you want to go to Seers' Keep," scoffed Craig. "You fancy yourself as a sorceress! Madame Caroline, palmist and fortune-teller, raiser of spirits and dabbler in the occult..."

"It's not about that!" Carrie said hotly.

"So what is it about?"

"It's about making choices," she said. "About personal integrity and moral responsibility, and everything else that matters in Irriyan and Llandor. It's about accepting we're here and wanting to do the best we can for ourselves and this world. It's also about stuffing your face with dead flesh when you don't have to!"

"A couple of helpings of fish stew is hardly a crime!" Craig retorted.

"Maybe not," agreed Carrie. "But we don't need to bring the corruptions of our world here, do we? And if you're prepared to go against Llandor in that, then what else are you prepared to do? If you refuse to go to Seers' Keep and get caught by the Grimthane, will you hand over everything you know? Sooner or later you're going to have to face things, Craig! You're going to have to accept you're here and decide where your loyalties lie – knuckle under and begin to toe the line!"

Craig hated her then. He hated her piety, her purity, her holier-than-thou attitude that found him lacking. He hated whatever it was in her that had prompted her to take on Gerwyn, that dared to believe she could one day become a seer and achieve parity with women such as Keera, or Delbeth, or Grandmother Holly. He hated her for thinking she could make a difference to whatever world she was in. And most of all he hated what she did to him – her crushing superiority that reduced him to the level of a worm or a rat. Knuckle under and toe the line, she said. Incensed, he rose from his seat and hurled the dish at her feet.

"Don't preach to me!" Craig said viciously. "From now on I'll do what I want and go where I want! And it's none of your damned business, right?"

"Wrong," said Carrie.

"What do you mean, wrong?"

She looked at him calmly.

"If what you do and where you go endangers Llandor, then it will always be my business," she said softly. "Remember that, Craig, next time you're called upon to choose."

"Don't threaten me, you pompous cow!"

"Now now!" chided Mrs Grinnipik. "Whatever it's about, we don't want it aboard the *Sea Sprite*! Captain Grinnipik keeps a happy ship, and harmony among the crew is the first order. Here's clothes for you both, the best I can do. Get yourselves dressed and I'll show you to your berths."

Muttering to himself, Craig pulled on the massive sealskin breeches and tightened the drawstring belt, donned a vest as huge as a nightshirt and a navy-blue sweater on top. It was orc-sized and reaching almost to his knees, but he was glad of its warmth when he followed Carrie and Mrs Grinnipik up on deck.

The north wind bit as he made his way astern, and the sunlight sparkling on the sea could not alleviate its chill. White horses danced in their wake and Avaron was gone beyond the horizon, although on the port side the coastline of Llandor was still visible – bleak rugged hills, sheer cliffs and rocky coves, grey stone villages nestling around tiny harbours. Flotillas of small boats fished the coastal waters and, astern and to starboard, other tall ships were sailing, driven southwards as the *Sea Sprite* was by the wind singing through its sails.

"A fine day for a departure," Mrs Grinnipik said cheerfully. "And the last it will be this season, I dare say."

"Why's that?" asked Craig.

"None sail this coast during winter," the orc wife informed him. "It's then that the Cape of Storms lives up to its name."

Carrie, garbed in a canvas shirt, a heavy woollen skirt in multicoloured stripes and a cloak to match, pulled up the hood and shivered. "It can't be winter already!" she protested.

"'Tis not far off," Mrs Grinnipik declared. "And a taste of it we've had already. Holed up in Avaron for nigh on a week we've been, waiting for the wind to veer and abate. I fear we'll be running the gauntlet as far as Seers' Keep, my dear."

Winter, thought Craig, the cold air laden with a promise of snow and ice. He had been in Llandor for over a year, and in the world he came from probably five years or more would have passed. If he went home now his schoolfriends would likely be scattered, grown men with families, ageing while he stayed young. He could no longer wish to return there. His chances there were gone and the life he had dreamed for himself was over. He had no choice but to do as Carrie said – accept that he was here, knuckle under and begin to toe the line.

Yet something within him, the deep inner core of himself, refused to do it. It was for him the ultimate failure, but what else was there? he wondered. Where could he go, apart from Seers' Keep? How could he live and for what purpose?

All over again the terrible trapped feeling churned inside him. He felt sick with it, sick with the desire to go back where he belonged and the knowledge that he never could. He wanted to lash out, to destroy Llandor, destroy this world, break it, smash it in sheer hate, sheer despair – or take it over, change it, alter it, do whatever he could, something, anything to make it more bearable. And, pausing before a polished oak door that gave access to a cabin beneath the poop deck, Mrs Grinnipik nodded.

"I've put you in with the White Mage," she informed him.

Craig clenched his fists. The scar on his face tightened, and the feelings he held in check were about to explode. He would not be pushed around any longer! But once again Carrie answered for him.

"I'm not sure it's a good idea to put Craig in with Gerwyn," she stated. "Neither of us like him, and nor do we know what his intentions are towards us."

"Oh dear," sighed Mrs Grinnipik. "I don't know where else Craig can go. The *Sea Sprite* was built to carry cargo and three two-berth cabins are all we have. One of those is Captain Grinnipik's and mine, of course."

"Couldn't he share with me?" asked Carrie.

"And where will I put the poor sick elfin lass?" asked Mrs Grinnipik.

"I'd rather have a hammock anyway!" Craig said angrily.

"Well, that's easily done," Mrs Grinnipik declared.

Craig turned away. Nothing was settled as far as he was concerned. Nor would it ever be as long as he remained in Llandor. "Now, let me introduce you to Nyssa," he heard Mrs Grinnipik say to Carrie.

"Nyssa?" Craig swung round, saw the look of incredulity on Carrie's face that reflected his own.

"That's her name," Mrs Grinnipik confirmed.

"Poor little lass, all on her own and sea-sick, too. She'll be glad of some friendly company, I'll be bound."

"But she should have reached Seers' Keep weeks ago!" said Carrie. "And is Gwillym here too?"

"You mean you know her?" Mrs Grinnipik asked in amazement.

"It's probably a coincidence in the name," said Craig.

But when Carrie opened the door he glimpsed her face in the gloom. She was pale and ill but she was unmistakably Nyssa. He saw her flaxen hair spread on the pillow, the recognition in her eyes, the joy in her smile. She reminded him of Irriyan, of something lovely that had once existed and was now irredeemably lost. Her frail hands reached out, but not for him.

"Carrie!" she croaked. "Delbeth said you would come! We were to wait for you in Avaron, she told us. Are Janine and Gwillym with you?"

"I thought Gwillym was with *you*," said Carrie.

"He was," murmured Nyssa. "But he found he couldn't leave without Janine after all. He went to back look for her, and I waited on my own, and this was the last ship leaving…"

Carrie closed the door and Craig heard no more. She had shut him out, out of her mind and out of her life. Alone with Mrs Grinnipik and a horde of orcs, in a world that was not his, Craig remembered what Delbeth had said. In the end you will always arrive where you are meant to be, the elf seer had told him. He would go to Seers' Keep, but it was nothing to do with choice and never had been. Quite simply, there was no other place to go where he would be safe.

CHAPTER NINE

The weather remained fine and blustery, and Carrie saw little of Craig during the first days of their voyage, just once at twilight watching the orc sailors haul in their fishing net, and again the same evening sitting nearby on an upturned bucket as they gutted their catch. The sailors sang as they worked, but Craig stayed silent and apart, willing to eat the results of their labour but not attempting to help. A lantern hanging from the yardarm cast shadows on his face. He needed a shave and a haircut, she noticed, but he departed below deck as she approached and gave her no chance to speak.

After that, and according to Mrs Grinnipik, Craig spent most of his time brooding in his hammock, as moody and uncommunicative as the White Mage. And most of Carrie's time was spent in the cabin with Nyssa, holding the sick bowl and sponging the elf girl's face. Meals were brought to them on a tray, although Nyssa seldom felt well enough to eat, and only when Mrs Grinnipik took over did Carrie go out on deck to stretch her legs.

She loved being on board the *Sea Sprite*, loved the friendly bustle of the ship, the deep bass voices of the sailors, the glints and tints and colours of the ocean, the music of the breeze through the rigging and the white billowing sails. It was wild and exhilarating being on a tall ship riding the elements, at one with the power of the wind and the power of the sea. Leaning on the bulwarks, gazing at the distant coastline of Llandor, or out across the open ocean, Carrie felt strong and invigorated as if she, too, shared that same power.

"You need to go outside, too," she told Nyssa.

"I can't!" wailed the elf girl.

"You can't stay walled up in here all the way to Seers' Keep!"

"Carrie's right," insisted Mrs Grinnipik. "'Tis out of touch you are with all that gives you life. A breath of fresh air will make you feel better."

Finally, Nyssa went out on deck and breathed in the wind and the sun and the salt sea air. Slowly her face regained its colour, her limbs their strength, and soon she was able to laugh and converse and eat a hearty supper. And 'twas a pity, said Mrs Grinnipik when she came to take away the empty plates, that Craig did not shift himself to do the same.

Carrie began to suspect that Craig was avoiding her, that he had turned against her as he had against Llandor and Irriyan and Seers' Keep. Leaning next to Nyssa on the bulwarks, she watched a school of porpoises leaping alongside the ship. Craig did not know what he was missing, she thought. Even the White Mage, who was equally anti-social and seldom spoke to anyone, still maintained a connection with the wellsprings of life.

Stationed on the poop deck with his pale robes fluttering and the wind dragging at his ginger beard and hair, Gerwyn, too, leaned on the bulwarks and stared out to sea. It was not the first time Carrie had noticed him there, gazing fixedly at some midway point between the ship and the horizon. There was nothing to see except the ragged shadows of clouds on the grey sea swell, but then Gerwyn was not really intent on seeing. Instead he was feeding, drawing strength from everything around him.

Suddenly, Carrie became aware of the effect he had. It was a kind of depletion, an erosion of energy. The vitality she had felt a few moments ago was somehow lessened, as if he had leached it from her. She had experienced it before on their journey downriver, had felt weakened and diminished by his presence, but now she understood the reason. Gerwyn did not share with anyone, he took. He took from people, drained and undermined them, took from the forces of nature, bent the elements to his will and used them to serve him. Concentrating, murmuring, drawing on the power of the sea and the sky, the White Mage was building up his strength.

"He's a parasite," Carrie muttered.

"Who?" asked Nyssa.

"Gerwyn," Carrie said darkly. "He sucks the life out of things!"

"You must be imagining it," said Nyssa. "He's the White Mage, Carrie!"

They had had a similar conversation before in one of Nyssa's more lucid moments. The elf girl could not believe that Gerwyn harboured any ill intent. He was the White Mage, she claimed, as powerful as Kadmon and far more trustworthy, his loyalty to Seers' Keep as unquestionable as Delbeth's. And if he had raised the sea and tested Carrie's abilities, he had done it for a purpose.

But Carrie retained her suspicions. And did she imagine the sea was growing rougher, the wind blowing stronger, the clouds darkening with her thoughts? A sudden squall of icy rain came sweeping in from the ocean, and the wind whipped up the waves, snatched away Nyssa's thin elven cloak and carried it seawards like a great silver bird. Overhead, stormy petrels screamed and circled and landed in the rigging.

"Furl the mainsail!" Captain Grinnipik cried.

The *Sea Sprite* wallowed. Queasy feelings stirred in Carrie's stomach and Nyssa turned green, heaving as the seas heaved and heading for the cabin. Gathering up the heavy woollen skirt she was wearing, Carrie followed. Inside was warm and enclosed, quiet compared to the noise without, no sound but Nyssa's harsh breathing, her anguished moan as she reached for the bucket.

"I can't bear it any more!" the elf girl whimpered.

This time Carrie knew how she felt. The day turned dark and the storm grew worse. Wind and rain lashed at the cabin window. The seas rose, and the ship rolled, and she was as sick as Nyssa. Her stomach emptied. Her muscles ached from retching. Bile stung her throat. It was all Gerwyn's doing, she declared. His sorcerer's power had drawn the elements to him, conjured a tempest that threatened to swamp them all.

"There there, my dear," Mrs Grinnipik murmured. "Grinnipik will brook no magic aboard his ship. Such weather is no more than we expect near the Cape of Storms and worse than this the *Sea Sprite* has encountered in her time. We shall come through it, never you fear."

"Unless we die first!" moaned Nyssa.

The orc wife stayed with them that night, her great warm bulk overlapping the stool on which she sat. Her face was grey and monstrous in the swaying lantern light, an alien creature more fish-like than human, yet Carrie was glad of her presence. The soft swift click of her knitting needles was as comforting as a heartbeat among the sounds of the storm that battered the ship, a metronome sound lulling her to sleep.

She awoke as Mrs Grinnipik departed. Grey morning light filtered through the cabin window and the storm had somewhat abated. She needed to go outside, she thought, escape from the smells of sickness and fill her lungs with air. Donning the heavy woollen cloak, clinging to the berth to steady herself, she opened the cabin door.

Then the storm struck again with renewed force and even Mrs Grinnipik, for all her sturdy bulk and great flippered feet, could barely stand against it. With her heart in her mouth, Carrie watched as the orc wife fought her way through the wind and rain to gain the safety of the hatch. Mountainous seas showered the ship with spray. The masts creaked and the sails were furled and none were on deck who did not have to be, only the captain unseen on the poop deck above her, his great voice booming in the wind – and someone standing in the lee of it, as Carrie did, a few metres away in the next cabin doorway. Just for a moment she glimpsed him – the pale flutter of his robes as he lowered his hands and completed his spell – before she backed inside and closed the door.

Now she knew for sure Gerwyn was responsible and, although she had begun to trust her own small powers, she lacked the strength to calm a tempest or even try. All day the storm continued and she was trapped in the cabin with Nyssa. The elf girl grew weaker, too feeble even to turn her head. Her dry lips cracked and bled. Her eyes were ringed by shadows, and her face was grey. She could keep nothing down, not even water. By nightfall, when Mrs Grinnipik returned, she was barely conscious and Carrie's anxiety had turned to anger.

"It *is* him!" Carrie said furiously.

"Get some of that food down you," Mrs Grinnipik advised.

"I saw him outside this morning casting a spell!"

"Who?" asked the orc wife.

"The White Mage!" said Carrie. "He's created this storm!"

"Why would he do that?" asked Mrs Grinnipik.

"I don't know," said Carrie. "Unless he doesn't want us to go to Seers' Keep and is trying to stop us?"

Lantern light threw flickering shadows on the cabin walls, and Mrs Grinnipik's pale fishy eyes fixed on Carrie's face. It was time to level with her, thought

Carrie, time to tell her all that had happened since she and Craig came to Llandor. The orc wife listened, and her immense dolphin-like grin turned strangely grim.

"So you fear there is treachery aboard?" Mrs Grinnipik said curtly. "You fear the White Mage works not for the Seers but for the Grimthane? That he intends to take Craig to Mordican and will use whatever means to waylay or turn this ship?"

"Yes," said Carrie.

The orc wife rose ponderously to her feet. "I'll go and consult with Grinnipik at once," she said wrathfully. "Mage or no, he'll wring the truth from Gerwyn. And if 'tis as you say, he'll be slung in the cargo hold out of harm's way until we dock!"

The cabin door banged as she left and Carrie waited, listening to the creak of the ship's timbers and the wind screaming in the outside darkness. Then, with a mighty sound of tearing wood, something broke. The *Sea Sprite* tipped dangerously. The lantern fell and smashed, filling the cabin with a stink of fish oil as Carrie doused the flames. Cries split the night. All hands were on deck in a chaos of movement until the ship finally righted itself and was back on course.

It was several hours later, after Carrie had wept and feared the worse, that Mrs Grinnipik returned and she learned what had happened. The forward mast had snapped, smashed through the bulwarks and made a gaping hole in the galley. Three lives were lost and several orcs were injured. And although Gerwyn had been dragged from his bed and cross-questioned, he denied any part in it.

"So no one believes me?" asked Carrie.

"'Tis his word against yours," Mrs Grinnipik sighed. "And he's the White Mage, my dear. But we shall be keeping an eye on him, never you fear."

"What happens now?"

"We'll be putting into the nearest port to make repairs."

"Which is probably what Gerwyn wants," muttered Carrie.

"I'll take care of him," Mrs Grinnipik vowed. "I've relatives in Scurry. You leave it to me."

By morning the storm had blown itself out, and the White Mage slept in his cabin, his purpose fulfilled. The sea became tranquil and, under a clearing sky in the lee of the Cape of Storms, the *Sea Sprite* unfurled her remaining sails and headed for harbour.

Scurry was built round a sheltered bay, its lights at twilight reflecting on the darkening water, the sun setting seawards in a sky of fire. Huddled in her great knitted cloak, the hood pulled up against the cold, Carrie leaned on the bulwarks and watched as the ship docked at one of the stone-built quays. Injured sailors and bodies for burial were taken ashore and loaded onto carts, and dray horses hauled them away along the waterfront. The clatter of hooves on the cobbles faded into the distance, was replaced by music and singing, sounds of drunken revelry and raucous laughter that drifted from the unseen streets beyond the warehouses. But it was a sound on board that made Carrie turn her head.

Closing the cabin door quietly behind him, his robes bleached by the rising moon, the White Mage made his escape. Heading for the nearest gangplank, he hurried ashore, and strode across the lantern-lit wharf. Whatever Mrs Grinnipik had planned for him was too late now. In a mixture of fear and relief, Carrie saw him vanish up an alley between the warehouses without a backward glance. And Craig's voice beside her sounded unusually cheerful.

"That's got rid of *him*!" he remarked.

"For now," muttered Carrie.

"You think he'll be back?"

"I don't think he'll give up," Carrie said worriedly.

"Give up on what?" asked Craig.

"You," said Carrie. "And probably me as well. He won't want either of us reaching Seers' Keep. We know what he is, don't we?"

Craig frowned.

"Maybe we're not meant to go there?" he suggested. "I mean, things have gone against us right from the start, and it's going to take weeks for the *Sea Sprite* to be repaired."

"We'll find another ship," Carrie said confidently.

"With nothing to trade for our passage?"

"I don't remember Captain Grinnipik asking for payment before we came aboard," said Carrie.

"I bet Nyssa won't want to board another ship," said Craig.

Carrie was silent for a moment, watching the cargo being unloaded. Bales and barrels and great wicker baskets were humped onto the backs of stevedore orcs and carried to the nearest warehouse for storage. Once emptied, the *Sea Sprite* would be hauled to a repair yard, and for at least one night they would have to stay in Scurry. But after that...

"What are you trying to say?" she asked.

"It was something Delbeth mentioned," said Craig. "In the end you will always arrive where you're meant to be, she said. So if we're not meant to go to Seers' Keep..."

"We?" Carrie rounded on him. "You told me you weren't going to go there anyway!" she said accusingly. "And why haven't you left us already? You could have gone ashore and been halfway towards wherever by now! You've nothing to fear in Llandor except Gerwyn and the Grimthane, Craig, so you're not bound to hang around and wait for me and Nyssa, are you?"

"I've decided to come with you," Craig informed her.

Carrie looked at him. "In that case, let's get one thing clear. Nyssa and I *are* going to Seers' Keep. We'll get there somehow and nothing is going to change that! Right?"

"I wouldn't bank on it," Craig retorted.

Not bothering to reply, Carrie returned to the cabin to finish the elf girl's packing, but what Craig said troubled her. Things *had* gone against them ever since they entered Llandor and there were still several hundred miles of land or sea to cross before they reached their destination. Gerwyn the White Mage waited, and bad things happened wherever they went, and now Nyssa and Mrs Grinnipik were involved. Biting her lip, afraid for all of them, Carrie reluctantly disembarked. Carrying the elf girl's bag, she followed Craig and the orc wife and the sailor, who carried Nyssa piggyback down the gangplank and onto the quay, trailed up the narrow alley between the warehouses and into a bustling street.

Scurry was a cosmopolitan port where all the races of Llandor and Irriyan came together. Orcs and humans rubbed shoulders with dwarfs and elves, and even an occasional goblin. Ramshackle buildings flanked the pavements offering food and lodgings to suit every taste, from cavernous basements with open fire pits, to green ferny grottoes with grassy beds; from seal-steaks and chowder to candied fruits and wafer bread. Cooking smells wafted from countless eating houses, and warmth, light, and music flowed from the open doors of pleasure houses and taverns. Scantily-clad girls and painted madams, troupes of jugglers and acrobats and gaily-costumed dancers vied for customers. And Craig was propositioned immediately, a hand on his sleeve trying to draw him away.

After that he stayed close to Mrs Grinnipik as they wended their way through the crowds. He was afraid, too, thought Carrie, as afraid as she was and afraid to admit it. There was an atmosphere to the place, volatile and dangerous, an underlying air of menace. It reminded her of Lydminster on a Saturday night – full of drunken youths looking for trouble, unfriendly eyes noting her presence. Scurry was not the most savoury of towns, Mrs Grinnipik warned. The hand of the Fell One had a long reach, and as long as they stayed there they had best not associate with strangers, nor walk the streets alone after dark.

"How long *are* we staying?" asked Craig.

"Until Nyssa's fit to travel?" Carrie suggested.

"And I've made arrangements," said Mrs Grinnipik.

Their lodgings were in a side street, an orc-sized boarding house three stories high. Bay windows shone eerily in the moonlight, and a lantern hanging from the porch lit the pavement as they approached. It was kept by a distant cousin, Mrs Grinnipik said as she knocked at the great front door. Her name was Aubrina Shillikin.

"I shall be making enquiries as to the whereabouts of the White Mage," Mrs Grinnipik said grimly. "Gerwyn will be seen to before he makes any move against you. And we orcs will make sure you reach Seers' Keep safely, never you fear. But meanwhile, bide you here. Aubrina will ensure that no one troubles you."

The fat pinafored orc who drew back the bolts and ushered them inside was as warm-hearted and garrulous as Mrs Grinnipik herself. Craig was assigned a dormer attic at the top of the house, and Carrie and Nyssa put together in a room overlooking the street. The elf-girl was still too weak to climb the stairs, but the sailor willingly carried her, depositing her gently on an oversized bed before he and Mrs Grinnipik departed back to the ship.

At first Carrie felt as small as Nyssa in the huge bedroom. But after the candles were lit, the curtains drawn, and a log fire blazed in the hearth, it seemed somewhat cosier. Later, an orc serving-girl brought a ewer of hot water for washing and a meal of potato soup and crusty rolls on a tray. Clean and fed, with a warming-pan placed in the waiting bed, and the polished oak flooring solid and unmoving beneath her feet, even Nyssa felt better. The elf girl curled her toes before the fire.

"Land," she sighed happily. "Isn't it bliss?"

"Yes," agreed Carrie.

But her sense of wellbeing was very short-lived. Dressed in one of Aubrina Shillikin's voluminous nightgowns, Carrie blew out the candles and opened the curtains to let in the moonlight. It was then that she saw a small goblin shape loitering in a shadowy doorway on the opposite side of the street. A quick fear filled her, although she said nothing to Nyssa. But later, when the elf girl slept and she again checked the street, her fear increased. The goblin was still there, its huge pale eyes fixed and intent, keeping watch on the house.

Carrie slept little that night. Thoughts churned in her head. Someone must have followed them from the ship. Gerwyn, perhaps, or some unknown other who served the Grimthane – it hardly mattered who. In spite of Mrs Grinnipik's assurances, neither she nor Craig could safely remain in Aubrina Shillikin's lodgings. They had to escape, now, while they still could – leaving Nyssa behind. But Carrie knew she would be unable to find Craig's room in the middle of the night, so whatever they did they would have to wait until morning.

Despite her intention she slept late, not hearing the breakfast bell or Nyssa dressing. Fully recovered from her sea-sickness and elegantly groomed, the elf girl roused her before she went downstairs. Hastily and heedless of her looks, Carrie donned the massive shirt and heavy woollen skirt, dragged a hand through her unkempt hair and hurried after her.

The dining room was crowded with orcs staying at the lodging house, full of the noisy boom of their voices, the rattle of cutlery and crockery, and the pungent smell of kippers. The orc girl, serving at tables, directed her to a sunlit window bay where Craig and Nyssa sat. They were talking animatedly as Carrie approached.

"I know one thing for sure – that's the first and last time I ever go on board a ship!" Nyssa declared. "I shall walk to Seers' Keep if I have to!"

"Is that possible?" asked Craig.

"There's a way through the Marrans," said Nyssa. "It's not much frequented so we'll need to carry supplies. Hire a pack-horse, maybe."

"What about the hire fee?" asked Craig.

"Delbeth gave me gems to barter in case of an emergency."

"I thought they were worthless in Llandor?"

"Except in exchange for trading tokens."

Carrie took the vacant chair. The table was laden with toast and honey and a tureen of porridge, but she was not much interested in eating. Instead she lifted the lace curtain and peered into the street. Morning traffic of carts and people passed outside, and once again she was aware of being watched. It was not a goblin this time, but a man, a man with pale eyes and sandy hair, loitering in the same doorway. She had seen him before somewhere – and fear revived a memory from long ago, of herself and Janine being hounded through the streets of Droon by that same man. Then Kadmon had come to their aid, but now there was no one. Alone in an unknown town, far from their destination, she, Craig and Nyssa were trapped.

"So we could go wherever we liked and you'd be able to pay our way?" Craig asked Nyssa. "We could become anonymous, disappear with no one knowing, and live independent of anyone else?"

"Why should we want to do that?" Nyssa asked curiously.

Carrie leaned forward.

"If we *are* going to disappear we'd better do it now," she said softly. "We're being watched!"

Craig's face fell, and fear flickered in his eyes as he lifted the curtain.

"Over there," said Carrie. "In the opposite doorway. It's the same man Janine and I encountered in Droon. And last night it was a goblin who was watching."

Craig let the curtain fall back into place.

"They're onto us!" he said in alarm. "What are we going to do?"

"Who's onto us?" asked Nyssa.

"Keep your voice down!" hissed Craig.

"So who's onto us?" Nyssa repeated softly.

"The flaming Grimthane!" muttered Craig.

"Or those who serve him," said Carrie.

Nyssa turned pale. "I was right," she murmured. "I *did* see a shadow following you when you came to Delbeth's house!"

"But it's not you they're after," Carrie assured her. "You'll be safe enough here once Craig and I have gone."

"You mean you're going to leave without me?" asked Nyssa.

"You surely don't want to come with us?" asked Carrie.

"Don't be stupid!" said Craig. "Of course she doesn't want to come with us! But if you want to help," he said to Nyssa, "you can give us some of those gems. If we buy a couple of horses then maybe we can reach Seers' Keep before anyone realises we're gone."

Fear, Carrie thought grimly, was a great catalyst. In a single instant it had reversed all Craig's intentions of slipping away with Nyssa to live anonymously and erased his last objection to Seers' Keep. For him nothing remained except the need to run again. Then Carrie saw the tears waver in Nyssa's eyes.

"Surely you don't *want* to come with us?" she repeated.

The elf girl looked at her appealingly.

"I know I'm not very brave," she confessed. "But I'm even more scared of being on my own. And I want to get to Seers' Keep, too. I'll do whatever you tell me, Carrie."

"That won't be necessary," Carrie replied.

Craig rose to his feet.

"Oh yes it will!" he said wrathfully. "If she comes with us she'll do exactly what we tell her! And if someone ends up carrying her it's not going to be me! And I'm not waiting either! If you're not at the back door within five minutes, Nyssa, I shall be gone without you! And the same goes for you," he told Carrie.

The elf girl fled upstairs.

But Carrie shrugged.

"You don't have the guts," she informed him.

CHAPTER TEN

Craig opened the door of a large back sitting room and ushered Nyssa and Carrie inside. Multicoloured scatter rugs were laid on the floor and on either side of the empty grate were two orc-sized armchairs. A portrait in oils of a seafaring orc hung on the wall above. And the window opened onto a walled back yard where a latched gate led into an alley beyond. Quietly, Craig raised the sash.

"We'll go out this way," he decided.

"What's wrong with the kitchen door?" asked Carrie.

"If we leave without being seen then no one can tell."

"Surely we owe Aubrina Shillikin an explanation?"

"And Mrs Grinnipik, too," murmured Nyssa.

Craig glared at the elf girl. He was used to being challenged by Carrie, but Nyssa had never set foot outside Irriyan until a week or so ago. She had lived a completely sheltered existence and had no idea what they were up against.

"You're not thinking, are you?" he said scathingly. "Suppose whoever's watching the house decides to pay a visit? How long will it be before someone talks?"

Nyssa flinched and lowered her eyes, but Carrie was not so easily persuaded.

"Aubrina Shillikin wouldn't willingly help the Grimthane!" she argued. "Nor Mrs Grinnipik either!"

"How about unwillingly?" asked Craig.

Without waiting for her answer, he climbed over the sill and dropped to the ground, and she followed a few moments later, turned to catch Nyssa's bag and help the elf girl descend. There was a window nearby set almost below ground level and a flight of steps leading down to a basement kitchen. Crouched out of sight in the shadow of the house, Craig waited a moment, listening to Mrs Shillikin singing as she worked.

"This is silly!" Carrie murmured.

"You want to take over?" Craig asked her.

"Take over what?" asked Carrie.

"Running things!" hissed Craig. "Not the same having someone else in charge, is it? And now you know how I've felt for the last twelve months!"

"It's got nothing to do with being in charge!" said Carrie.

"Hasn't it?"

Craig shrugged. Keeping to the shadows of the yard wall he darted towards the gate, lifted the latch and escaped into the alley. And once again, with Nyssa at her heels, Carrie followed him.

"Where are we going?" she inquired.

Craig had been intending to head for the main street and mingle with the crowds, hunt out a livery stable and hire some horses, but from the yard of the Green Man tavern round the corner a small hooded form detached itself from the shadows. His stomach knotted in fear and dismay. He should have thought of that! He should have allowed for the possibility that the back of the house would be watched as well. Now his only response was automatic.

"Run!" hissed Craig. "It's another blasted goblin!"

This time Carrie made no objection. Without stopping to think, she turned and ran, Nyssa behind her and Craig bringing up the rear. Their footsteps pounded along the alley, away from the streets, and the docks, and the bustling heart of the town, the goblin scuttling after them like a grey oversized rat.

How far they ran and for how long, Craig had no idea. One alley led into another, others branched off to left and right, a warren of empty sunless passages between the backs of buildings which criss-crossed the streets. And even in the streets there were few people about, and those they passed, both orc and human, merely turned their heads to watch the chase and made no attempt to help.

Craig grew hot and sweating in his woollen vest and knitted navy-blue jersey. The sealskin breeches chafed his legs, and Carrie fared no better. Her skirt and cloak kept tangling round her ankles. Her chestnut hair was damp and lank and plastered to her head, and Nyssa's hair had fallen from its pins. Several times the elf girl paused to brush it from her eyes, paused again to shift her travel bag from one hand to the other or briefly regain her breath. Their pace slowed because of her and Craig became more and more angry.

"Shift yourself, will you?"

"I can't run any faster!" gasped Nyssa.

"You're slower than a constipated snail!"

Carrie relieved her of her bag.

"None of this is Nyssa's fault!" she snapped.

"I told you we should have left her behind!"

"It's you they're after, Craig!"

"So what do you want me to do about it?"

"*You're* in charge!" retorted Carrie.

She always managed it, Craig thought furiously, the put-down that left him feeling stupid or inadequate, a metaphorical slap in the face. And what exactly did she expect him to do? Yet again he glanced behind at their pursuer. The goblin was making no attempt to close the gap, he noticed, nor was it threatening to attack. It was simply following. Craig was tired of running, tired of being afraid. It was all he had known since he came to Llandor. He was trapped between the fear that lay behind him and the fear that lay ahead, fear of the Grimthane and fear of Seers' Keep, and not even he could go on running indefinitely. Sooner or later he would have to stop and face it.

By this time they had entered a squalid area of kilns and forges, sawmills and timber yards and back-street workshops – and gradually a plan formed in his mind. He was in charge, Carrie had said. And what could one small goblin do against the three of them? What could it do against *him*? A high wattle fence flanked a farrier's yard and the gates were open.

"In here!" hissed Craig. "Find somewhere to hide!"

Catching their arms, he bundled Nyssa and Carrie inside. Bright sunlight dazzled his eyes as he shoved them behind an upturned cart and cast about for something to use as a weapon. Opposite, in the shadow of the building, horses tethered to a railing snorted and stamped, and a clangour of noise came from the smithy. A forge fire burned in the dark interior. Snatching up a length of wooden shaft broken from the cart, Craig stationed himself behind the gate and waited. And, crouched where he had left them, Carrie and Nyssa watched with terrified eyes.

"What are you going to do?" called Carrie.

"What's it look like?" Craig retorted.

"You can't!" shrilled Carrie. "I won't let you!"

"Just keep out of the way!" Craig warned her.

She was too late anyway. Even as she rose from her hiding place and started towards him, a hooded face peered cautiously into the yard, and Craig swung. The first blow felled it. Its legs buckled and it dropped at his feet. The second blow cracked its skull. Its limbs twitched, but the third blow stilled it, and after that it was easy. Nyssa's demented weeping and Carrie's cries meant nothing to him. Her fingers frantically clawing his arm and trying to restrain him meant nothing either. He shook her off like an irritating insect. He wanted done with it, once and for all ... all his fear, all his anger, all his hatred ... all that dragged him down, got in his way, prevented him from being what he really was. In a huge upsurge of power Craig smashed the goblin's body to a pulp.

"That's enough!" roared a voice.

They were a head and shoulders shorter than he, but strong and stocky with it. Surrounded by half a dozen determined dwarfs there was little Craig could do. Hard hands held him, prised away his weapon, pinioned his arms to his sides in a vice-like grip. Craggy bearded faces, dark with smuts and slick with sweat, confronted him. Deepset coal-black eyes glared at him from beneath bushy brows. Great bulbous noses sniffed the air. Fair or dark, or grizzled grey, each one reminded him of Diblin in a raging temper. And the younger one with the red beard and brows reminded him of —

"Bannock?" said Craig.

"Let him go," the red-haired dwarf commanded.

"So it *is* you!" Craig exclaimed. "What are you doing here?"

"More to the point, what are *you* doing?" snapped Bannock.

Craig stared at the body on the ground.

Grey-green blood soaked the goblin's clothes.

And, white-faced, Carrie and Nyssa stepped forward.

"You killed it!" Carrie said accusingly.

"It was after us!" Craig said defensively.

"But you didn't have to do *that*!" she said in disgust.

He stared at her blankly, not knowing what she

meant. All he had done was kill a goblin, just as Roderick had killed the boggarts on Black Mere, and Kadmon had killed the rock worm. He had clinched their escape and saved them from being discovered, yet Carrie took him to task because of it, and Nyssa wept, and the faces of the dwarfs surrounding him reflected the same disgust, their enmity towards the whole goblin race seemingly forgotten. One went so far as to take off his apron and cover its body. Another went to fetch a sack.

"What will you do with it?" asked Carrie.

"Cremate it?" said Bannock.

"Poor little goblin," sobbed Nyssa.

"Hang on a minute!" Craig said furiously.

Bannock turned on him.

"I'd keep my mouth shut if I were you!" the dwarf advised.

"But it was working for the Grimthane!" Craig protested.

"That's no excuse!" said Bannock. "Most goblins work for the Grimthane! And murder is murder, even in Scurry!"

Craig was tempted to argue, but instead he diplomatically removed himself from the scene, joined the horses and leaned on the hitching rail as the dwarfs cleared away the evidence of his crime, disposed of the goblin's broken body in the forge fire and sluiced its blood from the cobbles of the yard. Dark smoke smelling of charred meat drifted groundward and he could not understand what the fuss was about. No one had accused Roderick of murder when he killed the boggarts. What was the difference?

He watched and waited as Nyssa, Carrie and the dwarfs conversed within the shadow of the smithy. He noticed the covert glances cast in his direction, the frowns and shaking of heads, the grim expressions. He supposed, as no one invited him to join them, they must be discussing him, a criminal in a land where there were no laws and no judicial system. The scar on his face began to tighten and the torrent of emotions so recently released started to return – fear, anger, hatred – of them, of Llandor, of this world where he did not want to be.

Then, in a sudden flurry of activity, the dwarfs parted company. Two hoisted the cart upright and bolted a new shaft into place. Another watered the horses, harnessed and bridled them, backed them into position and secured the traces. Another filled the cart with straw from a nearby loft, and yet another loaded hogskins of water and sacks stuffed with hay and oats. Supply hampers were brought from within and Bannock, minus his blacksmith's apron, climbed onto the driving seat and took the reins. Coloured gems glittered in the sunlight as Nyssa paid the carriage fee before she and Carrie clambered aboard.

All the while Craig had watched and no one spoke to him. Now it seemed they were leaving, and he was not included in their plans. They obviously intended to abandon him. Judged and condemned, he was being sentenced to survive alone in Scurry. With nowhere to hide and no one to help him he could have no hope of escaping the agents of the Grimthane who would still be hunting him. He was not sure what he felt. A multitude of emotions seethed inside him as Bannock flipped the reins. The cart turned in a tight circle and headed for the gateway.

"Wait!" howled Craig.

The cart stopped, but not for him. A grizzled dwarf rushed past him hauling a tarpaulin and heaved it on board. Shelter for the wind and weather, he explained, from the night's cold and all unwanted eyes. They may well have need of it where they were going. Carrie nodded, and Bannock glanced over his shoulder waiting for her command, but her grey indifferent eyes were fixed on Craig's face.

"We're going through the Marrans to Seers' Keep," she announced. "Are you coming with us or staying here?"

He stared at her. The tone of her voice suggested she no longer cared what he did, yet, as no one had ever done before, she offered him a choice. He knew, if he accepted, he would be agreeing to travel with her on her terms. Whatever happened on this last stretch of road, Carrie would never again allow him to take control, and never again would she follow him. But it was still better to go with her and Nyssa, and Bannock, than go it alone and fall into the hands of the Grimthane. However galling and humiliating it was, Craig had no alternative but to acquiesce.

"I'll come with you," he agreed.

The curt nod of her head gave him permission to board the cart. At her say-so, to protect them all from whoever might be watching the road, he had to lie in the straw and be covered with the tarpaulin. And all the while he hated her, her air of cool command, her self-assurance, all she said and did that made him into the liability he had once claimed Nyssa might be. Harness jangled, Bannock whistled up the horses, and metal-rimmed wheels ground on the cobbles as the cart pulled away. No one acknowledged that their present escape was due entirely to Craig, to the death of a goblin for which he had been condemned.

Hidden beneath the tarpaulin, out of sight and out of mind, Craig might well have ceased to exist. Their chatter excluded him although Carrie told Bannock of her experiences in Irriyan, Jerrimer's death and Gerwyn's duplicity that Nyssa still refused to accept. And Bannock in turn recounted his own journey from the moment he and Grifflin had parted company. Mostly uneventful, he had followed the River Avar southwards, on the Llandor side, then taken the coast road to Scurry. Then, seeking the company of his own kind and loath to leave them once he had found them, he had lingered in the forge at Scurry until that day.

"And would you have stayed there?" Nyssa asked him.

"I might," admitted Bannock, "had you not passed my way."

"You didn't *have* to volunteer," said Carrie.

"No," agreed Bannock. "But you reminded me that there's more going on in this world than just my own life, or the doings of the dwarven race. It's why I set out from Stonehast in the first place. To become involved."

Involved in what? wondered Craig. Nothing ever happened in Llandor. It remained unchanging, a stagnant unprogressive land. Peering through a crack in the cart, he glimpsed a row of squalid clapboard shacks with shingle roofs and gardens made of sand, the impoverished environs of Scurry where people struggled to survive. Rows of vegetables grew in mounds of rotting seaweed. Salted fish and sewage was spread to dry in the sun.

A woman sitting on a front porch sewed sealskin breeches for orcs, and a group of ragged children played games on the dirt road with stones and sticks. No Barbie dolls here, no skate boards and Lego sets, nor electric sewing machines. But if Carrie, Nyssa and Bannock, and everyone else Craig had met, cared as much about Llandor as they claimed to, they would surely do something about it – unlock the doors of Seers' Keep, let loose the accumulated knowledge and apply it to improve the lot of the general population.

The town petered out when they crossed the river bridge and headed south. Then the countryside took over, a blighted landscape of ancient sand hills overgrown with brambles and coarse brittle grass, a landscape of goats and hovels and cabbage patches, small sheltered fields growing oats and asparagus, and stands of pine trees sculpted by the ceaseless wind. The cart bumped and jolted along the unmade road, and Craig felt bruised all over in spite of the protective bed of straw, but no one gave him permission to come out of hiding. No one considered him at all, in fact. His presence beneath the tarpaulin continued to be ignored.

The girls and Bannock talked until the sun began to set and Nyssa, complaining of the cold, lifted the tarpaulin to search for her travel bag. It was just light enough for Craig to see how her face changed when she noticed him, as if she had bitten an apple and discovered something nasty inside. He was not quite sure if it was a look of distaste, or disdain, or even revulsion he saw in her eyes, but one thing was certain. If it took him the rest of his life he would repay Nyssa for what she did to him in that moment.

They stopped as darkness fell and camped in a sandy hollow surrounded by pine trees. Even then Nyssa could not bring herself to speak to him, although Carrie and Bannock behaved as though nothing had happened. Beneath winter stars, huddled round a small fire that gave no warmth, they shared a supper of cheese and bread and fruit. But what plans they made had nothing to do with Craig. He had done his bit, helped get them this far and slaughtered a goblin, and they could expect no more from him.

They slept eventually, the girls in the cart on a bed of straw, Craig and Bannock on the ground beneath it with only the tarpaulin to cover them. For Craig it was a fitful sleep at best. The increasing chill kept waking him, Bannock snored, and the tethered horses snorted and stamped. A red sky at dawn seemed like a warning.

Stiff and cold, Craig crawled out from beneath the cart and went to relieve himself. It was a wild and lonely place, where nothing lived or moved except himself and a bird in the fiery sky, black and small in the distance. A hawk, perhaps? Or maybe a crow?

Craig squinted into the gathering brightness, his heart hammering in sudden fear. There was not just one bird, but many – crows, wherever he looked in all directions, sailing the wind and searching the land beneath, and he was alone and exposed with nowhere to hide. He made a dash for the camp-site but was instantly spotted. A solitary crow came spiralling down from the overhead sky, landing with a soft flutter of wings among the upmost branches of a pine tree. Black beady eyes peered down at him. Merrigan's bird, there was no doubt, a messenger from Mordican ascertaining his whereabouts. He picked up a pebble and hurled it towards it… and another, and another, until finally it launched itself skywards again.

The crow's harsh cry and the rain of pebbles falling through the trees awakened Bannock from his sleep. The dwarf's red-bearded face appeared from beneath the cart.

"What was that?" he asked in alarm.

Craig hesitated. It was too late for caution. The crow had spotted him and knew where he was. But if Bannock told Carrie, Craig was likely to spend yet another day concealed beneath the tarpaulin. Deliberately, he stared around their campsite.

"What was what?" he asked.

"I thought I heard something."

"You must have been dreaming," Craig informed him. "Unless it was the wind in the trees, perhaps?"

In the freezing dawn there was little point in returning to sleep. Craig gathered sticks and Bannock rekindled the fire, cooked a pottage of oatmeal and woke Nyssa and Carrie. After they had breakfasted, fed and harnessed the horses, they took to the road again. This time Craig sat up in front next to Bannock and the girls rode in the cart. It was a chill bright morning full of wind and sunlight, and the sky clear of crows, although, later in the day, Craig thought he saw one high and far away, shadowing them from a distance. His fear reasserted itself, but again he decided not to mention it. By then the landscape was becoming more and more barren, baked earth and scrub and dry brittle grass, flatlands where the horizons shimmered in the noonday heat. Nyssa complained of flies, and thirst, and heat-rash. And all the while they travelled Craig kept a look-out, waiting for something that so far had failed to happen.

By mid-afternoon the landscape changed again. The flatlands gave way to a rougher terrain of sand dunes and canyons, high rocky cliffs and dry river beds. There were birds a-plenty here, hawks mostly, feeding on the lizards that basked on the rocks, and a horde of crows picking at a carcass killed by a fox.

Nothing suspicious about those crows, thought Craig, and neither Nyssa nor Bannock had any experience of Merrigan's army. But seeing them must have triggered a memory in Carrie, for when Craig turned his head he saw her watching the skies although she, too, kept whatever fears she harboured to herself.

The cart rattled and jolted along a stony track. Towards dusk, the temperature began to plummet. Craig shivered, and Nyssa in her thin elven clothes began to complain of the cold. Her querulous voice grew more and more tearful. She wanted to stop and make camp, wanted warm food and a fire. The wind, funnelling up the canyon behind them, blew dust in her face and her backside hurt from sitting in the cart.

"So get out and walk!" Craig muttered.

Bannock shot him a look. The road wound southwards into shadows, heading towards a narrow pass that led to the desert lands beyond. It would feel warmer once they were out of the canyon, said Bannock. There, where they would be sheltered from the wind in the lee of the crags, they would find a place to camp. It was not much further.

"But I'm so cold!" wailed Nyssa.

Carrie loaned her the heavy knitted cloak Mrs Grinnipik had given her, pulled up the hood over the elf girl's pale hair, and hauled the tarpaulin round herself. Not much further, Bannock repeated confidently, but as the rock walls narrowed and towered above them on either side, the ambush was sprung.

The horses reared as a great net dropped over them and the cart. Bannock roared and thrashed, Nyssa screamed, and Craig froze in terror. Several rough-looking men, armed with knives and hatchets, clambered down from various rocky ledges and closed in on them. They were obviously in no mood for talking. Bannock was despatched with a clout on the head that sent him crashing to the ground, and a man with pale eyes and sandy hair lifted the net and hauled Craig bodily from the cart.

From a rocky ravine further down the canyon, another man led a string of horses. Craig was trussed and bound and slung over the back of a sturdy pony, and a screaming Nyssa was treated likewise. By then Carrie had freed herself from the entanglements of the net, her useless cries echoing from the high rock walls.

"Let them go! Let them go!"

"What do we do about *her*?" one man inquired.

"Leave her," the sandy-haired man said curtly. "We've got the one we want, the girl wearing the coloured orc cloak. Cut the horses loose and leave her!"

"She'll die if we leave her here!"

"And that worries you?"

"She's a human girl, Ventris! I'm not into murdering my own kind! I say we take her with us!"

"Aye," said another. "We can put her ashore before we cast off, or dump her within walking distance of Scurry."

Ventris shrugged. "Very well," he snapped.

Craig hardly knew what happened next. The canyon was full of noise: Nyssa's screams and Carrie's cries, the milling of horses and the restless clatter of their hooves as the attackers remounted. And the two approached Carrie, but as they did so a pale nimbus of light glowed around her and when she raised her arms the wind shrieked, turning the dust into whirlwinds. A bird swooped from the dark air, wings and claws beating at the men's faces, and a white ghostly form came speeding along the canyon. With hooves and horn the unicorn attacked.

"Leave her!" howled Ventris. "Leave her! Leave her! She's a blasted sorceress! Let's get going!"

Carrie's gaze moved to Craig, and her raised hands were poised to strike as if she would now blast him out of existence. But as the horses wheeled and cantered away, her image faded into the darkness and distance, although Craig would never forget that vision of Carrie standing among the clouds of dust and light, a sorceress with two men dead at her feet and another standing beside her – Kadmon the Black Mage risen from the grave, his black robes billowing round him. The memory remained along with Craig's own terror, undimmed by the desert cold and the freezing stars and whatever fate awaited him.

Chapter Eleven

Carrie stood alone in the twilight. The sound of galloping hooves had faded, and Craig and Nyssa were gone. Gone, too, was the vision of Kadmon standing beside her, his awesome power that just for a few brief moments she had shared. She had almost done it, had raised her hands in readiness, about to destroy what the Grimthane wanted in a blast of light, but Kadmon's voice in her head had forbidden her. Instead she had let Craig go, knowing even as she did so that Llandor might one day reap the resulting destruction. And Kadmon's power had gentled in response. His dark ghost dimmed and left her. Now, in the wind and dust and gathering darkness, in the bone-biting cold of the desert night, nothing remained but the bodies of men sprawled on the ground, the unicorn that had slain them and Bannock lying injured beside the cart. She went to kneel beside him and he tried to rise.

"I failed you," he murmured. "I failed you, my lady."

"Hush," said Carrie.

His face was pale, his hair matted with blood. And somehow or other she had to move him, find shelter for the night and tend his hurts. For her own sake, too, she needed a fire and food and some place to sleep where she would not die of exposure. Without the orc cloak to cover her, her arms felt icy and her fingers were growing numb. She had to get them both out of that canyon. But the horses were gone and she knew, before she began, that she lacked the strength to carry Bannock or even drag him very far.

"Can you walk if I help you?" she asked him.

"I can try," he muttered.

Awkwardly, with his arm round her shoulder, Carrie hauled him to his feet. But the blow to his head had affected him and, almost immediately, his legs began to buckle. She lowered him to the ground again and gazed around helplessly, not knowing what to do.

And the unicorn gazed at her, moonrise reflecting in the dark depths of its eyes. Shoshuna had followed all the way from Elandril, crossed the River Avar and travelled countless miles of countryside to find her way here. No one could own a unicorn, Garriel had said, and Carrie knew she could never own Shoshuna, yet it was for Carrie that the white mare had killed, Carrie who was responsible for the blood that darkened the spiralling horn and splattered her coat. With a feeling close to revulsion Carrie stared at her, but Shoshuna had no conscience, no awareness of having done wrong. Only in her eyes was there a love that would do anything to protect the girl who gazed at her.

A great lump formed in Carrie's throat as she held out her hand. The unicorn responded immediately, trotted towards her and nuzzled her face, a warm living beast offering her the only hope she had. She had no need to ask. A kind of understanding flowed between the two of them and each already knew the other's needs. Yet there was a courtesy that had to be maintained, an outward show of respect. Carrie stroked the warm white nose.

"Will you help us?" she asked "Will you carry Bannock? Carry our things? Take us out of the wind?"

Shoshuna stamped and tossed her head.

And Carrie turned to Bannock.

"I'll walk, you ride," she said.

"*Her*?" said Bannock.

“Her name’s Shoshuna,” said Carrie.

Bannock had never encountered a unicorn before, but he sensed the sanctity of the creature. Unlike other equine species, Shoshuna was no beast of burden, and nor was she to be ridden lightly. But, unceremoniously, Carrie shoved the protesting dwarf onto her back, loaded her with the tarpaulin and the cooking pot, canteens of water and a few other essential supplies, and led her away into the night.

They did not go far. Beyond the narrowest point the canyon widened again and the great desert opened up. Moonlight silvered the distant sand dunes and the rugged escarpment behind sheltered them from the wind. Instinctively, the unicorn headed downwards into a gully where the ground still retained some of the day’s warmth. There Carrie set up camp, and Bannock watched helplessly as she fed Shoshuna a nosebag of oats and hay, gathered dry scrub and lit a fire, boiled a little water in the cook pan and tore up one of Nyssa’s night-shifts to cleanse his wound and bind his head. Flames and the night stars reflected in the coal-black depths of his eyes as she handed him a portion of cheese and bread.

“It ought to be the other way around,” he muttered.

“What do you mean?” said Carrie.

"Me serving you, my lady."

Carrie frowned. "That's the second time you've called me that," she said.

"It's what you are," Bannock said stoutly.

"No I'm not," she denied.

"But it's in you," he insisted.

"What is?" she asked.

Bannock nodded towards the unicorn.

"She knows it," he said. "Even in Irriyan few can tame a unicorn and few can ride one. It's for you she came and did what she did – what I should have done if I'd been quicker and had my wits about me."

"You would have killed those men, too?"

"For you, my lady."

Carrie felt shocked. Killings had happened before – Maeve and Yanalf dying at the hands of the nixies, Jerrimer in the jaws of the water-horse, Roderick slaying the boggarts in Sedgemarsh, Craig slaughtering the goblin – but those deaths had been to save Craig from the Grimthane. Now they were for her: two men gored to death and Bannock willing to commit murder.

"I should have recognised it in you before," sighed Bannock.

"Recognised what?" asked Carrie.

"Power," said Bannock.

Carrie shot him a look.

"But I haven't got any power!"

"If you say so, my lady."

"And stop calling me that!"

"If you say so."

They sat in silence for a while listening to the sounds of the desert – the soft chirr of a night bird further down the gully, the cry of a hunting fox, the crackle of the fire and the wind sighing over the distant sand dunes. Nearby stones splintered with the cold. And that was power, said Carrie. It was everywhere around them in the land and the high stars, in the weavings of the Seers and the great grid walked by the wandering mages. She could learn to access it, perhaps, and learn to channel it, but it was not hers.

"Except that I saw," said Bannock. "I saw him standing there, and the dust blowing through his robes. I buried him on the Kellsfell but you raised him. You raised the ghost of the Black Mage and called him to you. Necromancy, my lady. That's *your* power."

Carrie gazed at him in horror. It could not possibly be true! She could no more command Kadmon's wandering soul than Janine could command Gwillym. He was a free spirit, answerable to no one – at least he had been when he was alive, and why should his ghost behave differently? He wouldn't, she thought. He had appeared beside her for reasons of his own that had nothing to do with her. She rose and spread the tarpaulin on the ground, added brush to the fire.

"We should sleep," she said curtly.

"I'll keep watch," said Bannock.

"Shoshuna will alert us if anyone approaches."

"As you wish, my lady."

"Stop calling me that!"

"As you wish."

He kept watch anyway and Carrie lay sleepless in the darkness, shivering in spite of the warmth of the fire. What Bannock had said frightened her. The intimations of power frightened her. Wherever it came from, whatever its source – the land, or the Black Mage, or the web woven by the Seers – it was still hers to wield. Only she was not qualified to use it. She needed to reach Seers' Keep, needed to be taught. She could hardly go on relying on Kadmon's ghost to save her from her own failings.

But he would, she thought. He would guard her from herself as long as he had to, just as Bannock and Shoshuna would kill to protect her or die if they must. They would do it for Llandor, because they believed she mattered, that the land had need of her. And all she could do for them was continue to believe in herself and not let them down, no matter how afraid she was.

She slept at last and woke in the grey half-light of a freezing dawn when Shoshuna snuffled her face. A bright fire burned. Oatmeal porridge steamed in the cooking pot and Bannock seemed somewhat recovered, although his face looked drained and the bandage round his brow was stained with blood. She ate in silence, aware of her own guilt, the empty plate taken from her hand and cleaned with tussock grass, and all he must have done while she was sleeping.

"What are we going to do?" she asked him.

He nodded to the unicorn.

"You ride and I walk?" he suggested.

"We could return to Scurry," she said.

"Not because of me," Bannock said firmly.

"But it might take us weeks to reach Seers' Keep!" Carrie protested. "And you're still hurt, Bannock!"

"Then I'll heal as we go," the dwarf replied.

Red dawn burnished the sand dunes as they extinguished the fire, loaded their supplies onto Shoshuna's back and clambered out of the gully. And the wind struck them, funnelled through the canyon, filling the air with dust and sand. There was another sound, too, and distant drumming of hooves upon stone. Someone was coming, heading in their direction.

"Ride!" Bannock howled at Carrie, as he drew a knife from his belt and whirled to protect her. But he had no need. The unicorn nickered softly as if in greeting, and a solitary rider emerged from the dust, flaxen-haired and cloaked in silver. Carrie heaved a sigh of relief.

"It's only an elf," she said.

Bannock sheathed the knife. "What's an elf doing here?" he muttered.

Carrie waited as the rider tugged on the reins and stopped beside her. Blue elven eyes gazed down on her in total surprise, and it was not a horse he was riding, but a small brown pony, sturdy and shaggy and strangely familiar.

"Elvertine?" said Carrie.

"Carrie?" said Garriel.

"You two know each other?" asked Bannock.

Laughing, Garriel dismounted and hugged Carrie to him.

"What are you *doing* here?" asked Carrie.

"I followed Shoshuna," said Garriel. "And a merry dance she has led me! But I never dreamed..."

"Are Janine and Gwillym with you?"

"Gwillym?" said Garriel. "I thought he had gone to Seers' Keep with Nyssa."

"He returned to Irriyan to search for Janine," said Carrie.

Garriel's eyes clouded momentarily.

"Then maybe by now he has found her," he said. "She stayed behind in Greenlea to look after Jerrimer—"

"Jerrimer?" said Carrie. "But he's dead, Garriel!"

It was one more lie the White Mage had told. Shoshuna had swum across the river, headed off the kelpie, and enabled Jerrimer to escape. Torn and bleeding, he had crawled to the nearby village and the villagers had crossed by the ferry and carried him to the house of the elven healer.

"We'd lingered there, Janine and I," said Garriel. "And when Jerrimer arrived, too hurt travel to travel again for a while, Janine stayed to help nurse him and I set off down river looking for you and Craig. But what happened with you, Carrie? Where's Craig? And where's the White Mage Jerrimer said was with you?"

It was a long story, and Carrie shivered in its telling until Garriel gave her his cloak. His face grew grim as he listened.

"So Gerwyn is a traitor?" he murmured.

"Yes," said Carrie.

"And Craig and Nyssa have been taken?"

"That about sums it up," muttered Bannock.

"What are you planning to do now?" asked Garriel.

"Go to Seers' Keep," said Carrie.

"Alone? Through the Marrans?"

"Me and the unicorn will look out for her," Bannock said gruffly.

Garriel was silent for a moment. Small eddies of dust whirled round them and the wind sang across the distant sand dunes.

"Shoshuna belongs in Irriyan," Garriel objected. "And what about Craig and Nyssa? What will happen to them? Delbeth has been training Nyssa for many years. She was destined to be an elf Seer, one who will maybe take Delbeth's place when she finally departs from the Western Havens. And if Craig should fall into the Grimthane's hands..."

"Are you suggesting we should go after them?" asked Carrie.

"Surely we have to?" Garriel said passionately. "For Llandor and Irriyan we must needs rescue them both! What say you, Bannock?"

Bannock cleared his throat. "We dwarfs were ever a practical race, and never let it be said that a dwarf fears to do what an elf dares, but as you have sought my opinion I am bound to inform you that I cannot, even for one minute, contemplate such a hair-brained venture, Garriel! Not only do those men have fast horses and a twelve-hour start, but the odds against our success, if by some chance we should happen upon them, are not exactly favourable. We would be two against many, my friend, and yourself an elf untrained for such a battle."

"I'll fight when I have to!" Garriel said fiercely. "And we shall have Shoshuna with us!"

Carrie paled at the thought, and Bannock shook his head.

"That unicorn was not bred for such a bloody purpose! Nor do I think she will turn from her path to follow the likes of you and I."

"She will if Carrie does!" Garriel retorted.

Bannock bristled. "You invite my lady to risk her life on such a cause?"

Garriel glanced at Carrie and raised an eyebrow. "I know Carrie," he stated. "She is not the kind of person to turn her back on her friends. And Craig was more than just her friend, Bannock! If we don't rescue him then all she has been through, and all everyone else has been through, will have been for nothing! And afterwards," he said to Carrie, "we can return to Irriyan, take Shoshuna home and pick up the life we left behind, everything just as we planned..."

"What's past is past, elf!" Bannock said harshly. "No one can return to it! What you left behind will not be the same when you return! You lure my lady with a false promise there! And I have failed her once, but I will not fail her twice, nor fail this land. For dwarfs and elves and men, and all who oppose the Fell One and the forces of Mordican, it falls on me to guard her on her way. You do what you must, Garriel, but we go on to Seers' Keep... my lady, her unicorn and I."

"Your lady," snapped Garriel, "whoever you think she is, dwarf, will make up her own mind upon things! Tell him, Carrie!"

Garriel was tall for an elf and handsome, too, and she heard the appeal in his voice. Part of her wanted to go with him, wanted to return to Irriyan and forget. Bannock had made her into something she was not, assigned to her powers she would rather not accept, a destination that was inescapable. But people had died to get her this far and, faced with the final decision, the choice between Bannock and Garriel, she did not know what to do. But the decision was not hers to make. Red beard bristling with indignation on her behalf, Bannock turned his head, and his face grew pale as the bandage round his brow.

"Death and corruption!" wailed the dwarf.

Automatically, Carrie turned to look too. The bright dawn had darkened without her noticing and the rugged escarpment was gone. Between her and any desire she might have to go with Garriel, and crushing all hope of rescuing Nyssa and Craig, was a towering tornado of sand. And someone stood in the midst of it, a black robed figure with raised hands. Kadmon had come to make up her mind.

She barely remembered what happened next. Garriel hoisted her onto Shoshuna's back, screamed at her to ride, then shoved Bannock onto Elvertine and leapt up behind him. By then the white mare was away, ears flattened against the stinging wind, heading into the desert. Glancing back, Carrie saw the storm was pursuing her. Whirling sand stung her face with a thousand lacerations of pain and Elvertine was dim as a shadow some way behind. Sensing her need, Shoshuna slowed to keep pace.

"Don't wait for us!" yelled Garriel.

"Keep riding!" shouted Bannock.

"But we could lose each other!" shrieked Carrie.

"We'll catch up with you eventually!" yelled Garriel.

"Wherever you are we'll find you!" vowed Bannock.

"No!" wailed Carrie.

Wind and sand stoppered her cry and the unicorn made her own decision. Her stride lengthened and she picked up speed, outrunning the storm front that would swamp Garriel and Bannock and the pony. Still looking back, Carrie saw it happen. Their vague shapes vanished in a swirling cloud of sand and dust that spread and widened, blotting out the hills and the horizons and any chance of relocating them.

She clung despairingly to the unicorn's mane and let Shoshuna take her where she would. But even Shoshuna could not outrun the wind. All around it whipped up the sand. The sun became hidden, distances unseeable. Time and direction had no meaning. But on and on Shoshuna sped across endless miles, her hooves barely touching the ground, the desert a blur of sand and speed around her. On and on, with the cooking utensils clattering round her neck, water sloshing in the sealskin canteens, food supplies and the tarpaulin now and then slipping from her back. And if Garriel and Bannock survived the storm, how would they survive the desert? Carrie thought wretchedly. From thirst and hunger they would likely die before they found her. She should have stayed with them. They could have sought shelter in the lee of a sand dune, and even if they had been buried alive at least they would have died together. Rather that than she surviving alone to bear the loss of them.

And it was her fault anyway, she thought. If she had not been tempted to return to Irriyan with Garriel, Kadmon would not have raised the storm to prevent her. But would he do that? she thought. Would he sacrifice two lives simply to force her on towards Seers' Keep? No, she decided. So maybe she had done it herself? Maybe she *was* a necromancer, just as Bannock had said, using her power to raise Kadmon's spirit and unknowingly commanding him? Could she have done that? she wondered. And if she had would he have obeyed?

"No," she murmured. "Stop thinking like that!"

But the thoughts persisted. Once, without knowing how, she had wrestled with Gerwyn to control the sea – so why not the desert and Kadmon, too? Obliteration was what she had wanted.

"Stop it! Stop it!" she screamed.

The wind dropped completely at her words. Small eddies of sand drifted groundwards and the air cleared. Slanting sunlight of late afternoon dazzled her eyes. Coincidence, she thought, it had to be coincidence because if it wasn't…

"Stop thinking like that!" she repeated.

Shoshuna slowed to a leisurely trot, her hooves echoing on stone. And this was not the landscape Carrie had left behind. Stark and grey, she saw the ruins of a city spreading from horizon to horizon: wide paved streets and tumbled walls and crumbling buildings, gigantic bridges arching over dried-up rivers and colonnades supporting nothing but sky. She guessed what it was. A city built by giants, all that remained of a long-dead race, and nothing alive in it except for Shoshuna and herself, a few tussocks of dry grass growing in the crevices between the stones and a hawk hovering some distance away, the soul of the Black Mage watching over her, awaiting her command.

"No!" shrieked Carrie. "It wasn't me who raised that sandstorm! It couldn't have been me! But do something to help Bannock and Garriel, Kadmon! Please! Please!"

Fear of herself grew as she saw the hawk obey, dart away towards the desert to hunt for the dwarf and the elf. Or maybe she was imagining things? Maybe it was just a bird and not Kadmon at all? Nearby, a flight of crumbling stairs led downwards into darkness, and an eerie silence lay around her, unbroken by the sound of Shoshuna's steps on the dust.

Then, as the sun began to set, the whispering began, half-heard voices among the ruins. Things moved among the shadows, pale glimpses at the corners of Carrie's vision that vanished when she stared. She had the power of necromancy, Bannock had claimed, power to raise the dead. But it was not she who commanded the wraiths of the Marrans – they obeyed a greater power than hers. Their sad, almost subliminal singing that welcomed the gathering darkness and the coming night welcomed her, too, a terrified girl alive and alone in a city full of ghosts.

They wanted her… wanted her… she could feel their desire. Their cold sad song seeped through her mind, remembering their defeat and their dead. She began to remember her own dead: the wolves, Benna and Festy and Yanalf; Maeve with her red-gold hair whom Jerrimer had loved; Roderick and Umla and Rikkin, perhaps, and Kadmon buried on the Kellsfell… all of them dead or gone. She had thought it was for Craig they had given their time and their lives, but it was for her, too, and the land that had called her to which she and they belonged.

And now Bannock and Garriel were lost in the

desert and Shoshuna was exhausted, panting and sweating and stumbling over mounds of fallen masonry, her boundless strength being slowly drained away from her as the dusk deepened and the wraiths continued to sing. They wanted the unicorn as well as Carrie, wanted their souls to serve the Grimthane, the Fell One, their Lord and Master, he who had led them once and led them still, who would wreak revenge for their dying. They sang of a future when giants would return again to Llandor, reclaim and rule the land that long ago had been theirs. And Carrie would help them...

Shuddering, Shoshuna stopped walking and, numbed out of feeling, Carrie sat astride her, staring across an open square to the ruins of a temple. There, gilded by sunset, a stone effigy squatted, a gigantic semi-human shape with clawed hands and tusked face, blind eyes eroded by the weather – Asgar, once worshipped as a god in Llandor, and worshipped still in Mordican, according to Umla. And the wraiths' song rose, a hymn of ecstasy that would bind her for ever to war and blood and slavery. She would learn to wield her powers and use them to kill. The unicorn, too.

"Fight them, Carrie!"

The voice was Kadmon's voice, and overhead the small hawk fluttered.

Carrie struggled.

"Choose, Carrie! Choose! Do not give in to them! You have the power, remember? Now use it!"

"No!" she murmured. Then, "No!" she screamed.

"For Shoshuna, for Llandor, use it! Use it!"

The wraiths and Kadmon battled for her mind. Black and red, blood and darkness, beat in her head. She could barely think, barely see, she was just a scrap of being lost among a terrible cacophony, the wailing of the wraiths and the bird that was Kadmon, its shrill wild cries urging her on. She had the power… she had the power… she could feel it in the land around her, feel it within her… red, black, dangerous, flowing through her bloodstream, about to kill.

"Use it! Use it!" the Black Mage cried.

"I daren't!" cried Carrie.

"You have to! You must!"

"Leave me alone!"

"Use it, Carrie!"

She released it in a blast of anger, a blast of blue light, power without control, which swept from her raised hands outwards into the sky and across the land. The statue of Asgar split and fell, its tusked face smashing on the paving stones beneath it. Softer, the thud of the hawk as it hit the ground, its small torn body lying there in the ensuing silence, pale feathers sheened by the light of the rising moon. The wraiths were gone and so, too, was Kadmon. Only Carrie remained. Carrie and Shoshuna, grief and absence – and someone standing behind them.

Sensing the presence, Carrie turned her head. Barely visible in the darkness a woman stepped from a broken doorway, her eyes bright with moonlight, her hair black as night.

"We meet at last," she said softly.

CHAPTER TWELVE

They rode all night at full gallop, the ropes chafing Craig's wrists and ankles, his whole body jolted and bruised. By dawn they had reached Scurry. Still trussed like Christmas turkeys, he and Nyssa were carried aboard a schooner and dumped in the cargo hold. The hatch was slammed shut, and Craig was left in the blind dark with the elf girl sobbing and retching as the ship set sail. Not until they were well out to sea did Ventris bring a lantern and cut them both free. Craig rubbed his limbs to restore the circulation.

"You're going to pay for this!" he said furiously.

The man's pale eyes flickered nervously.

"I'm only doing what I'm told!" he said.

"By whom?" asked Craig.

"Just don't give me no trouble," begged Ventris.

He left, and the hatch slammed shut again. Later a goblin lackey brought food and water, fish chowder that Nyssa refused to eat, and the scene was set for Craig's imprisonment. He was stuck for the duration of the voyage in a dark enclosed space with only a single lantern hanging from a hook in the ceiling shedding a swaying light, stuck where large rats scuttled in the shadows and the air stank of the toilet bucket and Nyssa's vomit and the bales of raw fleece on which they slept.

"Where are they taking us?" sobbed Nyssa.

"I'll give you three guesses," muttered Craig.

Days passed, and the elf girl was sick constantly, her moaning and spewing and snivelling driving Craig mad. And the ship rolled and wallowed through heavy seas, her timbers creaking and groaning. How long it had been since they set sail from Scurry he had no idea, and no one had told him where they were going, but Nyssa kept asking over and over again.

"Where are they taking us? Where are they taking us, Craig?"

"For Christ's sake, shut up!" he retorted.

He guessed, of course. They were being transported to Mordican, to Asgaroth, to the realms of the Grimthane, two prize imports among a cargo of fleece and wheat and barrels of grog – except that Nyssa was a mistake. It should have been Carrie who was with him. She was the girl who had worn Mrs Grinnipik's multicoloured cloak until a few minutes before they were ambushed, but no one had thought to remove the hood and check the identity of their captive, the moon-pale hair, the pointed ears, the fragile features that made Nyssa unmistakably elven.

He needed to do something, he decided. He couldn't stay helpless and powerless, dependent on the whims of others for the rest of his life. Sooner or later, before they reached Mordican, he needed to assert himself, and when Nyssa was sick again, his resolve hardened. He could not stand being shut in that stinking hold with her any longer. When next the bolts were drawn back and the hatch opened with a shriek of wind, Craig was ready.

The lantern guttered in the draught and a small goblin shape lowered the rope ladder and scrambled down. Light flickered in a pair of round milk-white eyes half hidden beneath a sealskin hood, gleamed on the blade of a dagger tucked in its belt. It regarded him warily as it approached, and had it known what he had done in Scurry to one of its fellows it would have been more than wary, nor for a single moment would it have turned its back. But it did. Craig leapt, and the goblin squeaked in terror as his forearm wrapped round its neck. The tray it was carrying, containing two dishes of chowder and a pitcher of drinking water, tipped onto Nyssa's lap, then crashed on the decking as Craig's free hand snatched its dagger and held it to its throat.

"Move and I'll kill you!" Craig threatened.

Ashen-faced, dripping with fish stew, Nyssa rose to her feet. "Please don't hurt it!" she begged.

Craig ignored her. The goblin needed to know he meant business. Greeny blood seeped from the first small cut and it had mingled long enough with humans to have learnt to speak their language.

"Don't kill I! Don't kill I!" it shrieked.

"If I let you go," said Craig, "will you do as I tell you?"

"Yes, master, yes," it said frantically. "Leto do whatever you say. Leto good servant, good goblin."

Knowing its name made it somehow personal but Craig could not afford to feel pity. He cut away the cord from the nearest bale of fleece and tied it round Leto's ankle. "You and me are going for a walk up on deck!" he said. "And don't try anything stupid because I'll be right behind you." Keeping hold of the leash, he gestured with the dagger. "Now move!" he commanded.

Leto crawled up the ladder ahead of him.

"Don't hurt him!" Nyssa repeated.

It was the last Craig saw of her for many weeks,

her face pale in the lamplight, her blue elven eyes gazing up at him in a final appeal before he stepped out on deck into a spume of rough seas and a windy twilight.

Brown sails flapped like gigantic birds and strained at the rigging and, unlike the *Sea Sprite*, there was no mess deck or cabins, just a canvas awning under which the sailors sheltered and slept and an open-ended galley behind the wheelhouse. The ship was heading northwards all right, northwards into the howling teeth of the wind, tacking across the ocean as if all the forces of nature were with her and not against her. Craig should have guessed who was in charge even before he spotted him: Gerwyn, the White Mage, positioned on the bows, his arms raised, his head bent in concentration, muttering a spell.

"Gerwyn!" howled Craig. "I want a word with you!"

One cowering insignificant goblin was nothing to bargain with, its fragile bony body no shield for the orc sailors' harpoons and Ventris's sword as they rushed to surround him. Except that if they were heading for Mordican, as Craig suspected, the Grimthane wanted him alive and wanted him for a reason. Against the White Mage and his crew, Craig was not quite powerless. Gerwyn might have the upper hand on board this ship but in the end he would be answerable for what he did. Craig shoved Leto aside. Defenceless except for the knife, he issued his challenge.

"Are you listening, Gerwyn? Tell your lackeys to lay down their weapons! And I want some decent treatment from now on! Put me back down there with *her* and you'll be responsible! It could be *her* throat I go for next time!"

The White Mage lowered his arms. His face twisted with rage as he made his way forward, and his voice was venomous.

"Who are you to give me orders, boy?"

Craig was aware of the sailors' unease, aware he could die in an instant from a blast of Gerwyn's magic, but he held his ground. He would not be intimidated. In the world he came from there was a power greater than magic, a power that could render Gerwyn useless. He smiled at the sorcerer's anger.

"I'm the one the Grimthane wants," Craig reminded him softly. "And when I get to Asgaroth, I shall remember you, Gerwyn."

His situation changed after that. Nyssa remained incarcerated below, protected from the threat Craig had made against her, and Craig himself was given the forward hold, provided with a change of clothes and water to wash in, and allowed up on deck, weather permitting. Gerwyn neither looked at him nor spoke to him again, but the orc who brought his meals was positively deferential and so, too, was Ventris. With an eye to the future, while still remaining Gerwyn's henchman, the scar-faced man had obviously decided to align himself with Craig as well.

"I just do what I'm told," he repeated.

"And yours not to reason why?" asked Craig.

"Quite," said Ventris. "You'll take account of that, will you?"

"I won't forget," Craig assured him.

And another thing he would never forget was the fear he felt, a dread rooted in the depths of his being that grew as each day passed. He could not imagine Mordican, and even less could he imagine the Grimthane, but hideous in his memory was an underground temple he had passed through in his journeying, the bestial image of Asgar whom the goblins worshipped as a god, its red eyes blazing, its stone limbs stirring into life. Or worse, the memory of the flesh-sharer who had briefly inhabited his body and controlled his mind, taken over Kadmon and driven him to his death on the Kellsfell.

He knew what would be expected of him. He would be expected to tell of the world he came from, all he knew of twentieth-century technology, take his place among the Fell One's minions, serve and obey. And he feared he would have no choice but to obey, feared as the days became weeks, as the weather worsened. Snow and sleet drove him below as the schooner made her slow way around the final headland and sailed up-river to Asgaroth.

It docked during the night and the following morning Ventris unceremoniously ushered Craig on deck. Nyssa was there already, shivering in the great orc cloak, the hood pulled up to hide her features, declining even to look at him or acknowledge his presence. Not that he cared, particularly. His whole attention was fixed on the land to which he had come and the feeling of sheer relief that washed through him.

Compared to his imaginings, and the realms of evil he had read about in books, Mordican was very ordinary – a sheltered valley between two chains of mountains. Asgaroth was as splendid as Elandril in its own way, and better by far than Droon or Scurry. It was a cold bright morning, snow on the peaks of southern mountains and the city crouching beneath them. It almost seemed familiar: grey stone buildings flanking the harbour, a palace in the distance with straight streets radiating from it, a towering coliseum, a templed acropolis. A Roman city, Craig realised in surprise. Eastwards, a viaduct crossed the river. And on the opposite bank in the lee of the northerly mountains, a lofty keep towered on a bluff and miles of rusting shacks housed the city's poor. Westwards, towards the river estuary where the water glittered like steel, were the industrial environs: tall chimneys spewing black smoke, steam and furnace fires, smells of sulphur and sounds of heavy machinery.

Again the relief washed through him. He understood Asgaroth, understood its mixture of beauty and ugliness. It was a birthplace of an industrial revolution such as Birmingham might have been a hundred and fifty years ago. There was nothing menacing about it, nothing threatening. Some way along the quay a bevy of hooded goblins unloaded cargo from another ship, a human overseer cracking his whip at the heels of a laggard, but even that Craig understood. It was part of the order of things, a natural order that Llandor denied, although he had little time to enjoy it.

"Bring them!" snapped Gerwyn.

Fear reasserted itself as, after a prod from Ventris, Craig followed Nyssa and the White Mage down the gangplank. He felt tempted to make a run for it, but Ventris gripped his arm and the smooth paved wharf beneath his feet swayed unsteadily after weeks at sea. Along with Nyssa he was bundled into a waiting carriage. The goblin driver cracked the whip and, with Ventris riding atop and Gerwyn to guard them, they went jolting and clattering along the wide avenue towards the Grimthane's palace. At least, Craig supposed that was where they were going.

The inescapable fear made him flippant.

"No spring suspension in Mordican yet?" he inquired.

"I'd save the clever remarks, if I were you," snapped Gerwyn.

But Craig noticed a tension in the sorcerer's face, an unease flickering in his eyes. It was a small consolation to know that Gerwyn was also afraid, and again, alighting in the palace forecourt before a vast colonnaded portico, he saw the slight nervous wringing of Gerwyn's hands as Ventris dismissed the carriage. And Ventris himself was paler than usual with droplets of sweat beading his brow. Only Nyssa seemed unaffected, as if somehow during the intervening weeks she had gone beyond fear, or discovered within herself a wellspring of courage. Head held high, the elf girl led the way up the flighted marble steps to the great front doors. Hauling Craig by the arm, the White Mage followed, still ignorant of Nyssa's true identity.

Gerwyn was incompetent, thought Craig. Or was it beneath him to lift the hood of her cloak and check her face? Whatever the reason, the Grimthane would not be pleased. And knowledge of such a vital oversight might be something Craig could use against Gerwyn in some future encounter.

Silently the doors swung open to admit them to the palace and, equally silently, closed behind them.

A pair of goblins in black and scarlet livery crossed halberds behind the small procession, to cut off their retreat. A pillared hall the size of a cathedral stretched before them, its rich mosaic floor swirling with colours, lit by the sunlight streaming through high arched windows to one side. On the other side was a balcony with smaller windows above it and doors beneath, the walls between draped with embroidered tapestries.

And it had to be there, of course – a statue of Asgar towering at the far end, its bestial features carved from snow-white marble, its ruby eyes glinting balefully in the light. And on a padded throne between its knees he saw someone sitting, a woman in a black cloak and gold gown. Their footsteps echoed as they approached and even at that distance Craig knew her, recognised the dark drifts of her hair, her amber eyes fixed on his face. All over Llandor and Irriyan, Merrigan had hunted him for her master and now, finally, she had him. He saw the triumph in her smile before Gerwyn thrust him bodily at her feet.

"He's all yours, Mistress!" the White Mage announced.

"Is he?" Merrigan said softly.

"I've brought him here, as you commanded!" Gerwyn said sharply.

"But he is not yet mine," Merrigan murmured.

Craig picked himself up.

"Nor do I intend to be!" he said furiously. "And stop shoving me around!" he told Gerwyn. "Your days are numbered anyway! With what I know, you'll be redundant in a couple of years—"

He ducked as the White Mage raised his hand, about to blast him but, quicker than he, Merrigan snapped her fingers. There was a flash of darkness as something shot from behind her chair and wrapped itself around Gerwyn's body. It was black, shapeless, smothering, nebulous as smoke, and through its eyes, red as glowing embers, Gerwyn's paler eyes stared out in terror. Nyssa gasped aloud, and Ventris retreated, and Craig, facing Merrigan, stood alone.

"My pet, the flesh-sharer," she informed him. "You've encountered it before, I believe. And shall I have it enter him and consume his soul?"

Craig swallowed. He might have gone along with seeing Gerwyn diminished. For the way he had lied and tricked and humiliated him, he thought it a just revenge, but he could hardly condemn him to death in cold blood. And he sensed the answer Merrigan was waiting for had nothing to do with his own desires or preferences anyway. He shrugged indifferently and tried to keep the tremor from his voice.

"If he's no further use to you," he said.

Merrigan laughed. "A strategist, no less! You are

more than we hoped for, Craig. Since our Roman centurion died we have long awaited such a talent. Our Master will be pleased, I think. And Gerwyn, for all his bungling, may yet prove useful – at least until your concubine is trained to replace him."

"She's not my concubine!" snapped Craig.

"No?" Merrigan raised an eyebrow. "Ah well, if the knowledge you bring with you from your own world is as powerful as you have intimated, we shall not need her talents long, nor Gerwyn's either."

She rose to her feet and once more snapped her fingers. The flesh-sharer withdrew, its smoky form slowly releasing the sorcerer and coalescing as a blob of darkness above his head. Its red eyes glared as the White Mage glared at Craig. They were sworn enemies now, although Gerwyn said nothing.

"Come," Merrigan said sweetly. "Let us resume our discussion in more comfort. There is someone I wish you to meet. And your retainer may remain here," she told Gerwyn.

Craig saw the relief on Ventris's face, then followed where Merrigan led, through a side door and into a large ante-room warmed by the sun and under-floor heating that shimmered above the vents. Embroidered lounging couches were set about, and low tables spread with bowls of candied fruits and sweetmeats and stuffed olives. A small portly man, wearing a black frock-coat and a stovepipe hat, stood beneath his portrait on the wall, and on the opposite wall hung another life-sized portrait.

Craig stared at it. It showed a Roman centurion, hawk-nosed and imperious, complete with leather skirt, metal breastplate and thonged sandals, a short sword at his waist and a plumed helmet tucked beneath one arm, a scarlet cloak flowing from his shoulders. And as he stared a memory began to stir… high hills at twilight, a Roman legion marching from the mists into the midst of a battle to fight with the giants and participate in their defeat. It was not his memory, yet he had shared it, watched through someone else's eyes as this same man, savage with anger, raged at the loss of his legion and vowed his revenge.

"Who *is* he?" he asked.

"Our Roman centurion, Marcus Aurinus," Merrigan replied.

Craig nodded. Suddenly he understood many things. A legend he had once read told of a lost Roman legion in long-ago England, and now he knew what had happened to it. He knew why Asgaroth seemed so familiar, why there were mosaics on the palace floor and underground heating ducts. On Earth the Roman Empire had crumbled. But in Mordican, at the instigation of a single surviving centurion who had fled across the Northern Mountains in a wake of a war, it had risen again and flourished.

Civilisation, social order, material advancement – the evidence was all around. It was not up to twentieth-century standards yet but it was a vast improvement on anything Craig had come across in Llandor or Irriyan. Goblin servants, hooded against the daylight, scurried to bring wine at Merrigan's command. Others, glimpsed through an open door, cleaned the courtyard round an indoor bathing pool, and in the air was a delicious mouth-watering smell of roasting meat.

Again Craig understood. Power... position... wealth... status... even roast meat – everything that was worth working for and gave life meaning, everything that added ease and richness and a sense of achievement, had been forbidden in Llandor and Irriyan. But Mordican offered it still. And was this the evil everyone feared? Was this the dreaded influence of the Grimthane that Seers and Mages fought against and common people were taught to shun? Was this what Craig had fled from? What everyone had tried to shield him from? The absurdity struck him and he wanted to laugh.

He wanted to laugh, but he held it in check. Coming from twentieth-century England he knew the rules, knew how a hierarchical society functioned. Only the fortunate or the fittest, the strongest or the cleverest, rose through the ranks to the pinnacles of power. He recognised its dangers, too – men such as Gerwyn who would bring him down before he had even begun – Merrigan herself, who ruled by sorcery on behalf of her Master – and the fat little man in the stove-pipe hat who was staring at him curiously.

"This is William Knock," said Merrigan.

The little man nodded.

"From Staffordshire, England, 1865," he said brusquely.

"Mr Knock is an inventor," said Merrigan. "He has given us machines driven by steam that possess the strength of many goblins. He will be able to verify the worth of what you know."

"Will he?" said Craig. "I somehow doubt it. He's not a scientist, is he? And I've seen no evidence of any great advancements in Asgaroth, no electricity, no internal combustion engines, no oil refineries. Mr Knock hasn't even provided you with the know-how for manufacturing muskets – and that's been around since the Civil War!"

Merrigan looked taken aback.

"Anyway," Craig went on. "I don't do deals with underlings. I'll deal with the Grimthane himself or no one at all!"

Nyssa gasped at his words, and Merrigan's amber eyes narrowed, and William Knock looked somewhat peeved, but no one spoke. The silence grew threatening, and Craig could smell his own sweat, but, as he had done on board the ship, he held his ground and refused to be intimidated.

"Well?" he snapped.

"The Grimthane sees no one on demand!" snarled Gerwyn.

"That's if he even exists," Craig retorted.

It was a kind of challenge and Merrigan put down her wine glass. "Very well," she said curtly. "Come with me. You too, girl," she said to Nyssa. "It is fitting, perhaps, that you should meet our Master. Your youth and enthusiasm will give him heart, mayhap, and for all the centuries we have survived we are not immortal. Inevitably the old must be replaced by the young some day. Is that not so, Gerwyn?" The White Mage shrugged and Merrigan chuckled. "Stay here with my pet and ponder on your own mortality," she instructed him. "You, also, Mr Knock."

Her gold gown swept the floor and her black cloak swirled at her heels as once again Craig followed her, across the courtyard by the bathing pool and into the darker depths of the Grimthane's palace. The scent of roasting meat grew stronger, wafting up a stairway from the basement kitchens with a clamour of noise and the shrill chittering of goblins that gradually faded into the hushed silence of a long dimly-lit corridor. It was as high as a church, a series of classical arches diminishing into the distances ahead, and great closed doors opened into countless unseen rooms on either side.

Craig's sea-boots, provided by Mrs Grinnipik, made an over-loud clatter on the smooth stone floor, and drowned the patter of Nyssa's elven slippers as she walked beside him. He saw her shiver, saw her draw the heavy orc cloak closer round herself, as if she sensed the presence she was about to enter and feared or loathed it. She was as stupid as everyone else in Irriyan and Llandor, thought Craig, conditioned to hate what she did not understand. But when Merrigan opened the door he, too, wanted to draw back.

There was a smell in the room. He was aware of it the moment he entered, a sweet, sickly, rotten smell, a smell of disease or death that made him want to gag. It hung like a miasma in the air, suffused the darkness, mingled with the acrid smoke of a candle that was the only light. Drapes were drawn across the windows and shapes within blackness loomed about him until his eyes adjusted. He was staring at an immense fourposter bed, at an elderly woman in a white apron hunched on a stool beside it who was obviously a nurse, and a withered ancient form beneath the sheets that had once been a giant. How tall he would have been in his youth Craig found it hard to tell, between three and four metres, perhaps.

But he was shrunken now, old, enfeebled, dying, although not yet dead.

"Master?" murmured Merrigan.

The massive head stirred on the mounded pillows.

"I've brought you the boy, Master."

The Grimthane's breath rattled... rheumy eyes opened and saw... and Craig recoiled. It was not Mordican that was evil, the land between the mountains where those defeated in war and exiled from Llandor had settled, nor the palaces and temples and burning furnaces of Asgaroth. Evil was a power within people, the essence of every soul that embraced it, and it gazed at him then through the Grimthane's bloodshot eyes and smiled in the toothless grin.

"Good," whispered the Grimthane. "Very good, Merrigan, my dear."

"And the girl, too," Merrigan went on. "She is strong in sorcery, Master. I can feel it. She will serve Mordican well when I have taught her." She grabbed Nyssa's arm and hauled her forwards into the candlelight. "Take off your hood, girl! Show the Master your face!"

Craig held his breath as Nyssa obeyed. The fairness of her skin was almost translucent, seeming to shine in the darkness, and an aureole of light glowed around her moon-pale hair. She was small, fragile, unmistakably elven – but there was nothing fragile about her spirit. Her weakness that Craig had despised was replaced by unflinching courage, and her blue eyes blazed as she faced the aged giant.

"I will never serve Mordican!" Nyssa said fiercely. "And nor will I ever call you master!"

The elderly nurse cowered as the Grimthane heaved himself up. Anger more terrible than Nyssa's twisted his features and spittle flew from his tongue.

"What trickery is this, Merrigan? Do you so desire my throne that you bring this elven spawn to hasten my dying? For more than a thousand years I have lived to plan the downfall of her race and reap my revenge on Irriyan and Llandor! And now, before the end, you think to face me with my failure that I may vent my spleen and follow my forebears into final extinction! But I will live long enough to curse you, shape-changer! My power is not yet gone!"

Nyssa backed against the wall as one gnarled hand lifted from beneath the bedclothes. And Merrigan grew pale. The dark air around her crackled with a thousand tiny points of fire. She shrieked as her hair singed, then changed her shape in response. Just for a moment the smooth mask of her face slipped, revealing the hag that dwelled beneath before her skin thickened and darkened, her nose became snout-like, her amber eyes grew small and red. Dugs swayed, and the bristles burned on her back, as the great black sow that was Merrigan wheeled from the Grimthane's wrath and charged from the room. Her voice was a enraged squeal that echoed along the corridor, shrill, maddened, intermingled with a woman's words.

"Damn you, Gerwyn! Damn your bungling incompetent hide!"

A smell of charred bacon remained… and the Grimthane lay exhausted against his pillows. Seizing the opportunity, Craig backed towards the door, froze as the great head lifted again and the giant's voice bade him wait. Bloodshot, malevolent eyes bored into his. He could feel the evil within stirring, reviving, drawing on his strength. He tried to fight it, but his head felt strange and muzzy.

"Are you worth all this?" the Grimthane rasped.

Craig struggled to answer.

"I must be," he croaked.

"Yes," echoed the Grimthane. "You must be worth it. Why else would Llandor expend so much energy and all their resources to keep you from me? Were you no use to them, the Seers would have opened a portal and bundled you out of this world as soon as you entered."

"What?" whispered Craig.

"Unless they have duped us all?" mused the Grimthane. "Unless it was the human girl and never you they wanted? Is it for her they let you remain in Llandor? A plaything for a future witch and not on your own account? Tell me the truth, boy! Speak, before I blast you from my presence!"

The Grimthane's mind released him and Craig's thoughts were once more his own. Rage boiled inside him along with a hatred such as he had never known before. Right from the beginning the Seers could have sent him home, could have held open the gateway in the Rillrush Valley or opened another, let him return to his own world and the life he had had there and never wanted to leave. But it seemed that they had kept him because of Carrie, kept him against his will, a consort for a would-be sorceress who had rejected him. The scar on his face felt tight and twisted and he could hear the venom in his own voice.

"They are afraid of me!" he told the Grimthane. "As afraid of me as they are of you! I have the knowledge to destroy them all! And Llandor and Irriyan as well! It may take me a while but I can unleash a power that's greater than all their magic! The power of a world where magic has ceased to exist! Guns, bombs, tanks..."

"No!" shrieked Nyssa. "You can't do that, Craig! You can't give into him! He's using you, don't you see?"

"And so did the Seers!" Craig said wrathfully.

"They used me to get at Carrie! Made me an exile from my own world! Trapped me here and wrecked my life! And I hate them! I hate them! I hate their flaming guts!"

Unleashed at last, his hatred swept through the room.

And the Grimthane smiled triumphantly.

CHAPTER THIRTEEN

After several months Roderick was used to it, the dank dingy prison, the communal holding cell in which he, Diblin and Dagda were confined. He was used to the lack of privacy, the smell of his unwashed body and the reek of the toilet bucket, the stone shelf against the back wall and the flea-ridden pallets on which he slept, the thin threadbare blanket that covered him. Above the sleeping shelf, a tiny barred window empty of glass let in a little natural light and, if Roderick stood on his sleeping pallet and craned his neck, he could glimpse a small strip of sky.

Nothing ever varied. Always the rattle of chains and padlocks, the semi-darkness of the corridor beyond the bars of the door, the wails and sobs of those who were imprisoned in countless other cells, the endless routine and the inescapable cold. Twice a day Jack Carrick, the jailer in charge, did the rounds, and twice a day the goblin warders slopped out, refilled the water jugs and food dishes. The food never varied either, lumpy porridge each morning, and bread and stew in the late afternoon. Only Roderick's fragile connection to the outside world, and Dagda's fingernails picking away at the mortar between the stones, kept alive the hope that he and the dwarf and the troll would eventually break free.

It was a slow painstaking task, two immense stones already prised loose below Diblin's sleeping pallet and others loosened behind them, but no glimpse yet of daylight through the cracks. Now as the warders' footsteps faded and Carrick, the jailer, turned the key in a distant lock, Dagda should have resumed her nightly quarrying, but the presence of a goblin, recently incarcerated with them, caused her to hesitate. Her eyes, glowing acid-yellow in the gathering darkness, looked questioningly at Roderick.

A succession of goblins had briefly shared their cell before this one. Most were old, and blind after years of working in the daylight. Of no further use and without families to care for them, they begged, scavenged or thieved until they were caught. Huddled in a corner or squatting on the floor, they were usually too feeble and apathetic even to be aware of what went on. But this one was younger and had its wits about it. And if under sentence of death, as most goblins were who landed in Asgaroth's jail, it was likely to tell what it saw in the hope of having its execution revoked.

"I say we leave things alone," muttered Diblin.

"It might be safer," agreed Dagda.

Roderick frowned. It would mean another night without progress, having to postpone their escape plans yet again. The ghastly stew of bones and meat gristle, which only the goblin had eaten with relish, congealed in his dish. Pale eyes gazed at it longingly, and Roderick knew that a gift of food was one way to befriend it. He pushed the dish towards it.

"Take it," he urged.

Its expression turned wary and its gaze flickered nervously from one to another – a human boy, a monstrous rock troll and a bearded dwarf, long-time enemy of all the goblin race.

"No one's going to hurt you," Roderick assured it.

Finally, the goblin crept forward. One clawed hand reached out and snatched up the dish of stew. Roderick saw lash marks on its face, lacerations shining with greeny blood, evidence of maltreatment, before it scuttled away again into the corner of the cell.

"Poor little devil," he murmured.

"But I still wouldn't trust it," growled Diblin.

"I suppose not," sighed Roderick.

Wearily, he took to his sleeping pallet, sat with his back against the wall and nibbled the precious chunk of dry bread. Sometimes this place got to him and so did everything else in Asgaroth – the poverty, the slavery, the deprivation – and men like Jack Carrick, human overseers with no kindness in them.

The jail was built on a rocky bluff and many a time, when Dagda hoisted him up, Roderick had seen through the window the miles and miles of goblin shacks spread out beneath him. He had smelled the fetid odours drifting across the city, the stench of tanneries, glue factories, rotting carcasses, droppings and dung. He had heard the death bellows of animals from a dozen different abattoirs, the sickly wail of goblin babies and the groans of the old. An aura of fear hung over this part of Asgaroth, an air of misery and hopelessness and perpetual menace. And in the distance, on the other side of the river, were the abodes of humans: white marble palaces, grand houses flanking tree-lined avenues, gardens and fountains.

Roderick had commented on it once, not long after he arrived. Gross and unshaven, Jack Carrick's face had leered at him through the door bars. It was the way things were in Mordican, the jailer had informed him, and how things were meant to be to, too. As an eighteenth-century footpad, he'd had his share of poverty, long years of hiding in the woods and living hand to mouth. But here men were favoured just for being men. Here Jack Carrick was rich, with a villa and servants of his own, and held in high esteem. Here, no one cared about goblins.

"You want to wise up, boy," Carrick had advised him. "It don't do to question what is, see? You could be like me, if you plays your cards right. Out of this place in no time. I can probably swing it for you if you give me the nod."

And now and then Roderick felt tempted. He could do nothing where he was but maybe, if he were on the outside, he could influence some changes? Have Dagda and Diblin released along with him, and salvage a few goblins maybe? But he doubted if he could go along with what might be demanded of him in return. He could pretend to grovel at Merrigan's feet, or falsely swear loyalty to the Grimthane, but he could never agree to policing the streets and ordering a few hundred more destitute goblins to their deaths, or organising work-schedules and driving hundreds more blind, or pressganging them into some factory farm or foundry, sentencing them to a lifetime of hard labour just for being born. Where goblins were concerned, the permutations of suffering and injustice were already limitless, and he would not add to them for the sake of his own release.

Depressed and shivering, Roderick moved, wrapped the tattered elven cloak closer around himself and paced the floor to keep warm. It was almost winter now. Outside, darkness had fallen early, and the lantern in the corridor guttered in the icy draught that blew through the high barred window. Inmates in the other cells moaned and coughed and settled to sleep, but the goblin, squatting in the corner, watched and listened.

"What about Umla?" Roderick murmured.

"Too dodgy," Diblin said instantly.

"She wasn't there yesterday," Roderick reminded him. "So she's bound to come tonight."

"We can't risk that felonious little worm-dump snitching on her and Rikkin!" hissed Diblin.

"And there's always tomorrow," Dagda whispered.

Roderick sighed and continued to pace the floor. He had once thought Umla had died on the mountains, yet another victim of Gerwyn's magic, but instead, when Merrigan took him, Diblin and Dagda captive and marched them to the city, Umla and Rikkin had followed and sought them out. He remembered the patter of stones being hurled against the prison walls, remembered Dagda hoisting him up to the window and seeing Umla there, her small goblin shape lurking in the shadows of the street below. How she and Rikkin survived alone and friendless in Asgaroth, Roderick had no idea, and Umla never stayed long enough for him to ask. Each time she came she was risking capture, risking her life and usually, after a few quick words, she departed. But seeing her was enough to set his mind at rest, enough to let him know she was still alive, watching with Rikkin for the moment they broke through the prison wall and waiting to lead them to safety. And he needed to see her now.

"Give me a bunk up," he told the troll.

"Don't be a fool!" hissed Diblin.

"I just want to know if she's there," whispered Roderick.

"And if that pointy-eared little creep should cotton on?"

"All I want to do is look out of the window!" Roderick said loudly.

Finally, the dwarf nodded. His need to know how Umla fared was as acute as Roderick's, and the goblin watched curiously as Dagda, compliantly, cupped her massive hands. Then, from the distance, came a series of familiar sounds: the key grating in the lock, the far door opening, Jack Carrick's boots and a patter of footsteps approaching along the corridor. They were bringing in a prisoner, an unscheduled intake at the wrong time of day. Instantly Roderick and Diblin took to their pallets and Dagda curled in her sleeping pose on the floor.

Shadows danced in the lamplight and the company came into sight with Jack Carrick in the lead and the prisoner, surrounded by an escort of goblin warders, following behind. They halted before the door of the cell and, selecting a key from the bunch at his belt, the jailer undid the padlock and removed the chain. He was grinning at Roderick.

"Here's what you've always dreamed of, boy! A nice little wench to keep you warm at night."

Bowing mockingly, he stood aside, and the girl entered. Except for the smallness of her stature, Roderick could see nothing of her. Her figure was clad in a great multicoloured cloak, her features hidden by the hood. But someone knew her. Shrieking and chittering, the goblin flew to her side, clutching at her cloak as the cell door clanged shut.

"Me not tell, Mistress! Me not tell!"

"Leto?" said the girl.

The hood slipped exposing her face: skin translucent as porcelain, bright blue eyes and slanting brows, pointed elven ears and a tousled mass of white-gold curls. Roderick gazed at her in awe, struck by her brightness, her beauty. She almost seemed to shine, a nimbus of light glowing round her as she bent to comfort the creature who tried so pitifully to comfort her.

"What they do to us?" the goblin whimpered.

"No one will hurt us," she assured it.

"Touching," sneered Carrick. "But don't count on it, miss. More likely it'll be hard labour or the rope for both of you."

Leto wailed and the elf girl bit her lip, a trace of fear flickering in her eyes. Then her chin lifted proudly. "Rather that than serve the Grimthane!" she replied.

The jailer laughed.

"Another muggins," he said to Roderick. "You two should get on well together." And, waving the guards into line, he turned and strode away. Their footsteps faded. The distant door closed and the key turned in its lock. Disturbed goblins chittered fearfully in the surrounding cells and silently the elf girl regarded her fellow captives. Her gaze moved from Roderick to Diblin and then to Dagda, taking in the troll's height and bulk, the craggy features, shaggy lichen-like hair and luminous yellow eyes. Even seated, Dagda was immense, and again the nervousness flickered in the elf girl's eyes.

"Dagda's a friend," Roderick said quickly.

"You've nowt to fear from any of us," Diblin said gruffly.

The elf girl relaxed. "My name is Nyssa," she said softly.

"What are you doing here?" asked Roderick.

"I was mistaken for someone else and captured," she said.

"And me not tell them," Leto repeated.

"I know," sighed Nyssa. "Had it not been for your loyalty I might have been thrown overboard weeks ago. But they were bound to find out in the end that I wasn't Carrie."

Roderick stared at her. A huge excitement gripped him at the mention of Carrie's name, only to be replaced a moment later by a wave of anxiety. "Carrie?" he said. "You know Carrie? Where is she? What's happened? Is she all right?"

"You know her, too?" asked Nyssa.

"I'm Roderick," said Roderick. "We came into Llandor together, Carrie and I. And she should have reached Seers' Keep ages ago! Craig, too! They can't still be on the run, surely?"

It was a long story Nyssa told, of her life in Irriyan and the elven city of Elandril, of Delbeth the elf seer to whom she was apprenticed. She told of a unicorn named Shoshuna, a rider named Garriel, and Kadmon's death on the Kellsfell. Janine, Gwillym, Jerrimer, Craig and Carrie had arrived in Elandril together, she said, but they had not left together. And Nyssa, who had set out with Gwillym for Seers' Keep, had known nothing of how they fared until she and Carrie met again on board the *Sea Sprite*.

Then it was Carrie's story she told, beginning with the plans she had made to stay with Craig in Irriyan and ending with the ambush in the canyon.

"I was cold," said Nyssa, "and Carrie lent me her

cloak. The men who ambushed us must have thought I was her because it was me they captured, me and Craig. We were taken back to Scurry and put on board another ship—"

"You mean Craig's in Mordican as well?" Roderick asked in alarm.

"Yes," said Nyssa. "He was at the palace when I... when Merrigan and the Grimthane found out who I was."

She paused and chewed her lip as she remembered.

"You've met the Grimthane?" Roderick murmured.

Nyssa shuddered.

"I was never very brave," she murmured. "And the Grimthane was—" She paused again. "I never knew what evil meant before that moment."

"Who is he?" asked Roderick. "What is he like?"

"He's a giant," said Nyssa. "An old, dying giant."

"I thought the war in Llandor had wiped out the giants?" said Roderick. "And how can a single ailing giant arouse such widespread terror?"

"You would know if you met him," said Nyssa.

"But what power does he possess?"

"Evil!" growled Diblin. "She's already told you that!"

"He feeds," murmured Nyssa. "Feeds on other people's feelings – fear, rage, hatred, pain, suffering. It makes him stronger. When he saw who I was his anger turned on Merrigan. She became a sow to escape him and almost gored the White Mage to death. She would have, if Craig hadn't stopped her. He said it wasn't Gerwyn's fault, that he might come in useful, and it was a bandit named Ventris who was responsible."

"And Ventris blame me," whimpered Leto. "He say I serve you on ship and I knewed all along you was elf not human. He say I should have told him, whip I bad and send I here."

Nyssa stared at the lash marks on his face.

"I am sorry, Leto," she said brokenly.

"Where's Craig now?" asked Roderick.

"Is he still free?" demanded Diblin.

Nyssa's expression hardened and her voice seemed cold. "I assume he is still at the palace," she said. "Merrigan obviously likes him well enough and the Grimthane, too. His hatred of the Seers is almost as great as theirs. They are looking to him as the new generation, just as Delbeth did with me. I should think he is free to demand whatever he wants and have his wishes granted."

"You mean he could get us out of here?" asked Diblin.

"If he wanted to," said Nyssa.

"Thank God for that," breathed Roderick in relief.

"Except that he was the one who ordered me in here," Nyssa said bitterly. "Somewhere out of sight and out of mind until he decided what to do with me, he said."

"What?" said Roderick.

"You sound surprised," said Nyssa.

"That's a bit ungallant even for Craig," said Roderick.

"You're saying we can't count on him?" asked Diblin.

Nyssa shrugged. "It probably depends on how he feels about you," she said. "He has never liked me very much."

"He not like goblins much either," muttered Leto.

And nor, Roderick remembered, had Craig been over-fond of him. But he could not believe Craig would refuse to help him if it was within his power to do so, nor would he leave Nyssa to rot in jail for the rest of her life, no matter how much he disliked her. Craig was not inhuman in the way Jack Carrick was, and he certainly was not evil. He might play along with Merrigan and the Grimthane, he would probably have to to save his own skin, but he was also clever enough, and ambitious enough, to make full use of the situation. He might bide his time, he might leave Roderick and Nyssa to sweat for a while and gloat on their powerlessness, but in the end he was bound have them released. Or was he? To the fat boy at Lydminster Comprehensive that Roderick had once been, Craig had shown no mercy.

"No!" Roderick said with certainty. "Craig's not that mean! He'll do what he can for us, I know he will."

"You had better be right!" Diblin said gruffly.

"We've just got to trust him, that's all," said Roderick.

"As I trusted Gerwyn," murmured Dagda.

Since Nyssa came the troll had listened in silence, but now she lumbered to her feet. If Roderick was right, all well and good, she said. If not, they had best trust themselves and be quick about it. Cupping her hands, she nodded to the high window.

"Tell her we'll be out tomorrow," she said.

"Tell who?" asked Nyssa.

"Umla," squeaked Leto. "She 'nother goblin, Mistress, 'nother pointy-eared creep like me."

"You were listening?" growled Diblin.

"And what if we're not out by tomorrow?" asked Roderick.

"Just tell her we will be!" Dagda insisted.

Hoisted aloft, Roderick peered between the window bars. The bluff, on which the prison was built, dropped a sheer ten metres to the street below, and the street was empty, the miles of goblin shacks black and white beneath the freezing moonlight. But foundry furnaces lit the far horizon and within the silence was a hum of sound, a murmur of voices like insects in a midden, and the distant alleyways scuttled with life. Then from a dark doorway crept a small shadowy shape and Umla's round white eyes gazed up at him.

"That you, Roderick?"

"We'll be out tomorrow!" he shouted.

And the goblin girl stuck up her thumb and slipped away.

"She'll be there," said Roderick as Dagda deposited him on the floor.

"How are we going to get out?" asked Nyssa.

The rock troll wasted no time explaining. Reaching beneath the sleeping shelf, she heaved aside the heavy stones she had so carefully replaced the night before. She was crazy, thought Roderick, there was no way she could be through by tomorrow. It had taken her weeks to burrow this far – slowly, relentlessly, picking away the mortar – and she was still less than halfway through the prison wall. But then, comprehending, Leto produced a knife, a fish-gutting knife, tucked in his boot, that the jailer had failed to notice, and Dagda was no longer alone in her task.

Throughout the night they took it in turns, loosening and removing the larger stones as the troll disposed of the rubble, scrunched it and swallowed it, her great gut grinding it to dust. They worked until they sweated, even Nyssa, and by dawn they had succeeded. Faint traces of daylight shone through the cracks and, with a few hefty shoves, they could have been free. All that remained was to shred and knot the blankets, fashion a rope to climb down the bluff.

But they had to wait for the night again and carefully, so as not to disturb the outer stones, Dagda replaced the granite blocks and filled in the gap, sat on the floor with her back to the sleeping shelf to hide the traces. The troop of goblin warders came to slop out and fill their dishes with porridge and, unbeknowing, Jack Carrick made his morning rounds. Inmates along the corridor and Leto, too, gibbered in fear as those chosen for execution were dragged away.

"Your turn tomorrow, goblin," the jailer said, grinning.

Nyssa's face paled as Leto whimpered and clung to her. And Roderick knew that for Leto's sake alone they had to get out that coming night and not wait for Craig to release them. But Craig came anyway, halfway through the afternoon, resplendently dressed in crimson velvet, with black leather knee-boots and a fur-lined cloak. Merrigan stood beside him in a gown of black and gold. His hair had grown since Roderick last saw him, blond locks that curled around his shoulders, freshly washed and shining in the lamplight, and there was a scar on his cheek that had not been there before. But his eyes were the same, an intense cold blue, sweeping imperiously over their faces.

The jailer fawned and grovelled.

"These are the prisoners you asked about, my Lord."

"I can see that for myself!" Craig said curtly.

"They are all well cared for, just as you would wish."

"You know nothing of what I wish!" Craig retorted.

Merrigan chuckled and his gaze moved on, dismissing each one in turn with a glance of sheer indifference, until he reached Roderick. After months in jail Roderick had no idea what he looked like, unclean, unkempt, his clothes hanging in tatters, he was barely human probably, but it was something other than his appearance that caused Craig's face to twist in an expression of loathing. Something old and unforgiven heaved to the surface, a hatred born of another world that reached back through the years. A cold sad feeling lodged in Roderick's stomach. If it had not been for him, Craig would not be here. And now, for all Roderick was and had been, for the journey through Llandor and a thousand imagined slights, Craig would make him pay.

"What will you have us do with them, Lord Craig?" Merrigan asked mockingly. "Will you plead clemency as you did with Gerwyn? Spare their useless lives? If so you should beware lest the Grimthane form the opinion that you lack the guts to warrant your position."

The scar on Craig's face tightened and whitened, and the hatred in his eyes was replaced by a flicker of fear, and for a moment Roderick felt sorry for him. Craig could command the life or death of all of them yet, in truth, he was even more powerless than they were and less free. But his voice betrayed nothing.

"*Are* they useless?" he inquired.

"Totally useless," purred Merrigan.

"I think you're wrong about that," Craig told her.

Merrigan arched her eyebrows. "You dare to disagree with me, Lord Craig?"

"When I have to," Craig said evenly.

"Then tell me your reasons," Merrigan said eagerly.

Craig shrugged. "If nothing else, they have a hostage value," he said. "Not the goblin and the rock troll, perhaps, but the others certainly. Carrie knows them, Merrigan. You have only to send Gerwyn with a message to Seers' Keep and she'll return with him willingly to save their lives. And we brought books with us into Llandor that could be useful. We can demand those too."

Merrigan smiled and her amber eyes shone.

"Good," she purred. "I am impressed, Lord Craig." She turned to Carrick. "You heard him, jailer! Do as you will with the troll and the goblin, but guard the others well! Now, lead us out of this wretched place. We have seen enough for one day."

With a swish of her skirts Merrigan was gone and, without even a backward glance, Craig followed. Their footsteps echoed along the corridor. The door clanged shut to the outer world and the key turned in the lock. The whimperings of goblins in the surrounding cells faded into a final silence.

"So much for him!" growled Diblin.

"He couldn't do anything else," said Roderick.

"He could have," said Nyssa. "We all have a choice, Roderick. In every moment of our lives we have a choice."

"Then maybe, one day," mused Roderick, "when the Grimthane dies and Craig takes over, he'll begin to make a difference here. Change things for the better."

"Do you really believe that?" asked Nyssa.

It was possible, thought Roderick. And if Craig was not free in any other way, he was free to choose, free to reject the Grimthane's ways and always would be. And as long as Craig was in Mordican, Roderick would not give up hope.

"At least he saved us from being executed," he said.

"He made no attempt to save Leto and Dagda," mused Nyssa.

"We were never going to be executed anyway!" Diblin said gruffly. "Merrigan brought us here for our hostage value in the first place! She was testing him, that's all! Playing him for a puppet and seeing what he was made of! And now we've *got* to get out of here! We've got to reach Seers' Keep before Gerwyn does and warn Carrie."

"And I must return to my tribe," said Dagda. "Put an end to our alliance with Mordican, our hostility for dwarfs and elves."

"But where I go?" Leto asked mournfully. "Where Umla and Rikkin go? Lands of sunlight no good for goblins and people no like us anyway."

"*I* like you," said Nyssa.

"But you go, Mistress," Leto said plaintively. "You go where I not follow. You go home and I has no home. Goblins got no place but Asgaroth."

Roderick frowned. Dark in his mind was the memory of a monstrous stone statue, a vision of Asgar the goblin god. The goblin race had been enslaved for centuries – generation after generation, cowed by giants and the demonic image they worshipped, ruled by their own terror. Now, in the teeming slums of Asgaroth, they served the Grimthane and knew no better. But Roderick knew. He knew where the goblins came from, where they belonged and where Leto should be – in the deep dark forests of Estnor, the sweet green gloom beneath the towering pines, little hunters as perfectly evolved as the wolves and the deer, bound like their fellow creatures to the woodland ways and living free. And, knowing that, could Roderick really return to Llandor and forget?

He would have to stay, he thought. Diblin and Nyssa could go to Seers' Keep, but he would stay. He would stay for Leto, a lifetime if he had to – running, hiding, surviving as Umla and Rikkin survived. He would stay until the last goblin was led out of Mordican, because, in the end, he could not trust Craig to release them, no matter how much he hoped. And the elf girl was watching him, her clear blue eyes fixed on his face, as if she knew.

"You're going to stay, aren't you?" she said.

"Yes," said Roderick.

"Stay where?" asked Diblin.

"In Mordican," said Roderick.

The dwarf bristled. "You needn't expect me…"

"I don't," said Roderick. "But someone has to help them."

"Help who?" growled Diblin.

"The goblins," said Nyssa. She put her arm protectively round Leto's shoulders. "We'll find somewhere, Leto, I know we will. We'll find a place where the land speaks to both of us."

Roderick's heart fluttered. "You mean you're staying, too?" he asked her.

Nyssa smiled. "Nothing happens by accident," she said. "We choose, and if our choice is wrong things go against us. It seems I was no more meant for Seers' Keep than you and Craig were, Roderick. And how can we leave if Mordican is where we are meant to be?"

Roderick grinned and glanced up at the window. Darkness was falling, a wet wind whining round the heights on which the prison was built, and a cold draught whistling through Dagda's hole in the wall. Just supper and lock-up to come, a rope to fashion, and then he would be free – free to begin with Nyssa the life they had both inadvertently chosen.

CHAPTER FOURTEEN

For Carrie the long journey was over. Only she and Shoshuna, with Merganna to guide them, had come through the Marrans alive. The bird that had borne Kadmon's soul was dead and search parties sent from Seers' Keep had scoured the desert for weeks but Garriel, Bannock and Elvertine the pony had never been found. She had grown used to it now. The acuteness of her feelings had diminished to a dull ache, the loss of them mingled with all the other losses – with Maeve and Roderick, Craig and Nyssa, Gwillym and Janine.

But there was no death except of the body, Merganna told her, only a passing from one world to another just as Carrie had passed from her world into this one. And there were some, Merganna said, who possessed the power to access those other worlds and cross the boundaries between dimensions. Some who could glimpse the shades of the so-called dead and hear their voices; who could raise phantoms, command and control the ghosts that lingered where once they had lived, bound by love or hate to a particular person or place. Mayhap, said Merganna, Bannock had been right and Carrie had that power. Mayhap the shade of the Black Mage would return at her bidding. It was impossible to know what powers she possessed until she was tested. And for that, said Merganna, she had to be willing. It had to be she herself, not the Seers, who wanted to know.

"The land needs who the land calls," Merganna reminded her. "You are come to this world for a purpose, Carrie, but you are not obliged to accept it. You can do as most have done before who happened here – leave Seers' Keep and seek some other life – or else do as Gwillym intended, wait on a portal to open and risk returning to the world you left behind. Think on it anyway. We grant you time and freedom and all else you may need until you have made up your mind."

Alone, Carrie pondered as the weeks slowly passed. Sometimes she visited the stable block where Shoshuna was housed, roamed through the narrow streets of the town to the harbour or the causeway that led to the mainland. And sometimes she explored the island, wandered along the cliff tops or combed the sandy beaches. There was no sign of winter at Seers' Keep. Flowers and creepers cascaded over its buildings, tall trees threw flickering shadows on its whitewashed walls, and the sea was turquoise, the surrounding horizons dissolving into a haze of light.

Sometimes, Carrie could feel the power of the island rushing into her and pulsing through her bloodstream. Her skin prickled. Her nerves tingled. Her head filled with flashing colours. But she did not want it, was afraid to own it, afraid of what it would make her into – not herself but someone else, someone important – a seer, a sorceress, elevated, deferred to. She tried to ignore it, tried to contain it, power held within her that had no outlet except through the pain of a monstrous migraine.

She kept to her room after that, high in the tower in the coolness of the great keep, a self-imposed prison with a balcony overlooking the sea. Days grew long and lonely and she began to feel more and more isolated and apart. She saw nothing of Merganna, nothing of anyone she could speak with, apart from the dwarf girl, Angarran, who cleaned her room and brought her meals on a tray.

Red-haired and sturdy, Angarran acted as a

servant and added to Carrie's sense of uselessness, although Angarran herself did not see it that way. Dwarfs, said Angarran, were a practical race, mostly incompetent at magic and not much suited to academic learning. She preferred the conversations of the kitchen quarters to the abstract discussions of the classroom, and domestic tasks were more enjoyable than long hours of study.

"We can't all be seers," Angarran declared cheerfully. "It takes all sorts to make a world and what I do is as valuable as anything Merganna does. By serving the Seers I serve the land, and so do we all, one way or another."

"All except me," murmured Carrie.

"You will," Angarran assured her. "Those who don't serve the land and all that lives in it serve the Grimthane instead, and I can't see you doing that."

She bustled away and once again Carrie was alone with her thoughts. Unlike the twentieth-century world she had come from, the land mattered here, was important to everyone. But if Craig told the Grimthane what he knew – and he might well be forced to – then Llandor could change. The forces of Mordican, armed with tanks and guns and modern weaponry, could take it over. And Llandor would become as England with its forests cut down, its marshes drained and put to the plough, motorways and traffic linking its towns.

And its towns would spread, grow to become cities, great urban sprawls of Droon and Scurry and Kellshaven, their inhabitants working in office blocks and factories, control of their lives no longer their own. Wolves would be exterminated. Great tracts of land would be buried beneath concrete with its power inaccessible, its magic slowly dying.

"No!" said Carrie. "That can't happen!"

But it might, she thought, if Craig supplied the know-how. And why would he hold back? It was what he had talked of throughout the journey, what he had wanted from the moment he came to Llandor: flush toilets, hard roads, a transport system, antibiotics, hamburgers, progress, modernity. He hated Llandor as it was, hated everything about it. It was people living in the Dark Ages, according to Craig. And a shadow followed him, a vision of the world from which he came that he would gladly impose on this one. And if the Grimthane provided the means...

"No!" said Carrie. "Craig wouldn't do that!"

But her thoughts insisted that he might.

As yet it was only a suspicion that Craig might betray Llandor, but Gerwyn already had. And had Merganna believed her? she wondered. The word of a girl against the White Mage, and all her witnesses gone or dead? He could return, she thought, denounce and deny her and reclaim his place among the scheme of things. Unless by then she had gained a place for herself, a position of power and trust that was greater than his?

The power filled her. Colours beat in her head. The land had called her and Kadmon had died for her. Shoshuna had killed for her and Bannock had sworn to serve her with his life. She had been no one in the world she came from, someone whose existence would have made no difference to anything, but here, as with the land itself, everyone mattered. And she knew she had to accept herself, learn to use whatever powers she possessed to defend Llandor against Craig and the Grimthane and Gerwyn the White Mage who would destroy it.

"You are ready, Carrie?"

The voice of the Enchantress came softly from behind her. Eyes, green as moss, fixed on her face as Carrie turned round. Merganna was standing in the doorway, her dark hair stirred by the breeze from the sea, her green robes shimmering with light. Behind her was Angarran, the dwarf girl, grinning cheerily, a silken russet gown draped over her arm. Neither Angarran nor Merganna had any need to ask. Somehow they already knew. Carrie was ready for the final testing, ready to assume her place in a battle that had not yet begun.

Deep within the keep a calling bell rang, summoning the seers to their places. And dressed in the russet gown that reflected the chestnut highlights of her hair, Carrie followed where Merganna led – down a spiral staircase, along dim corridors, down again and along another corridor, through a small back doorway and into a vast underground council chamber.

It was cool and dark, lit by candles in sconces that shed a flickering light. Great arched doors were closed at the far end and tiered seats, empty except for the few who had been called there, rose behind her and on either side. In the centre of the floor space was a large pool of black water. Nervously, Carrie approached it, stood on the edge of it, a round lightless abyss deep as a well into which she could fall and fall for ever. It reminded her of Delbeth's scrying pool, reflecting nothing, not even her face. And that was exactly what it was, Merganna said, and its depth was an illusion, the bottom of its basin no more than a hand-span beneath the surface.

"Do not be afraid of it," Merganna said. "What images form will indicate what powers you may possess and where, within Llandor, you future may lie. And always remember it is yours to command."

"You mean I have to scry for myself?" asked Carrie.

Merganna smiled.

"Were we to scry for you, Carrie, we would see

only a host of possibilities. It is you, and only you, who truly knows what you are capable of. We are gathered here to bear witness, that's all."

"But I don't know how to scry!" Carrie protested.

"I will talk you through it," Merganna replied.

Seers and mages looked down on her from the tiered seats, hunched forms perched and watching, their faces shadowy and indistinct. But their eyes glittered in the candlelight and she could feel the intensity of their stares. At her feet the dark water waited and the voice of the Enchantress spoke to her softly, stilling her fears.

"Let go of yourself, Carrie. You are safe in our midst and no harm can come to you. Let go of your thoughts and your emotions and fix your eyes on the pool. Concentrate your mind upon the blackness of the water, concentrate your attention. Know that the pool will obey you, that you will see what you need to see, and watch the images arise… watch them… watch them…"

Nothing happened at first. All she saw were the reflections of the candles, pinpricks of light distant as stars in a midnight sky. Or maybe they were not reflections? Maybe they really were stars, pulsing stars of differing sizes, differing brightness, some remote and alone, some so close together she could barely distinguish one from another. Then the water turned grey, and it was not only stars she could see but pinpricks of darkness as well that merged into blackness at the far side of the pool.

"I don't understand," she said.

"It is too soon yet for understanding," murmured Merganna. "Keep your thoughts at bay, Carrie, and observe what happens."

A core of radiance shone at Carrie's feet and a fan-shaped web of fine glowing lines spread outwards across the grey surface of the water linking the brighter stars together. Within the web the greyness varied. Here and there were areas of shadow and, on the left where the stars were more numerous, the spider-web lines became lost in a shining nebula of light.

"I still don't understand," said Carrie.

"Try looking deeper," Merganna suggested.

"How do I do that?"

"Concentrate. Will it. Focus your mind."

She did as she was bidden, fixing her gaze on the nebula of brightness, as if she would see into it, or through it, or behind it. And briefly she *did* see: Irriyan from a high place, its woods and plains and rivers spread out beneath her, the glow of its magic that all too quickly faded as the star grid reappeared. Again she focused her attention, this time on a bright conglomeration of stars away to the right, and again she saw: a town built of mellow brick, a market place thronged with people, riverside wharves, Droon with the snowy hills beyond it. It was gone in an instant, replaced by the star grid again, by her shifting stare that next revealed the waterfront at Scurry. And the areas of shadow gave rise to images of Sedgemarsh and the Marrans, Harrowing Moor and the ruins of Deep Dell – sad places, haunted places, places where bad things happened.

"It's a kind of map!" said Carrie.

"It is indeed," Merganna confirmed.

It was a map of the three lands, Llandor and Irriyan and Mordican, and those who inhabited them, their darkness, their light. When she gazed at the points of darkness the pool revealed nothing, but when she gazed at the stars a succession of faces swam into view: old faces, young faces, men and women, elves and dwarfs – Carrie did not know them. But the brightest stars were the seers and the mages – Seers' Keep the light at her feet and the fine spider-web lines the links of power that joined the others to it, with Keera among them in the Rillrush Valley, Grandmother Holly on Harrowing Moor, an old dwarf shaman singing over a pit of fire-stones. She could follow each of the threads outwards with her eyes and actually feel them, oases of power and brightness, centres of sanctuary in the land around them.

"The power of six," Merganna murmured. "Six the lines of power, the fan-shaped wedges walked by the wandering mages, though gone are the Black and the Silver, absent the White. And six times six, the nodes and intersections held by the Seers in their places, with some remaining vacant. Yet our power holds."

Carrie barely heard. Her gaze travelled across the pool to where the web of power faded in the darkness of Mordican. There were a few stars even there. No thread linked them to Seers' Keep but she could still see who they represented. Both joy and relief Carrie felt when she glimpsed Roderick's face and knew he was alive. She saw Nyssa and Diblin, too, and searched excitedly for Craig. But the star of his being failed to shine and instead she found goblins – Umla and Rikkin and others besides, even a rock troll, its acid-yellow eyes gleaming beneath the surface of the water.

Mordican was not all bad, she thought, just as Llandor was not all good. And here and there, as she followed the webbed lines outwards, she could perceive a thinning in their fabric, points where the links of power began to fray. Viewed from sideways on, the pool showed her cracks in the air, apertures of light or darkness similar to the vertical hold on a television set, rifts that widened and narrowed and vanished again as the power-links were repaired.

But as each crack appeared Carrie glimpsed another world directly beyond it and shadowy shapes of those who existed there. Had she known how, she could have opened a portal to admit them – shades, phantoms, people of her own world, departed spirits... and Kadmon, the Black Mage.

He turned his head, as if he knew she watched him, and her heart leapt. He was not dead or destroyed as she had feared. Elsewhere, as Merrigan had said, he continued to live. And whether it was his power or her own longing that opened the portal and allowed him to step from that dimension into this one, Carrie had no way of knowing. It simply happened. Next to her, with a small cry of astonishment, Merganna drew back, and a gasp and a murmuring rippled through the audience of seers and mages as Kadmon's ghost rose through the water and hovered above the surface, his black robes shimmering with light. Carrie could see him clearly in every detail – the smile that moved his lips, the candles shining through him, the laughter twinkling in his eyes. His words whispered in her mind.

"Magic conceals truth, Carrie, and the pool will not reveal what the Seers seek to hide. Look with your own eyes. Look at those who are around you."

She turned her head. The whole council chamber and everyone in it was bathed in light and the shock hit her. Everyone was old, every last one of them, seers and mages, their faces wrinkled and ancient, eyes shrunken in their sockets, their heads hoary, their bodies bowed and bent. Merganna, too, standing beside her, was a little old woman, stripped of her youth and her loveliness, the facade created by her magic. Carrie stared in horror until the light that was Kadmon sank into the pool and faded, and the slowly returning darkness restored their disguise.

Then nothing remained but the silence, the grid-map shimmering on the water and the appalled understanding Carrie had gained. They were all old, all the links in the web that protected Llandor, old men, old women, the shaman dwarf and the wandering mages, Delbeth the elf seer and Grandmother Holly – even Keera was no longer young. And with Craig's help, the Grimthane would create changes, the greatest threat Llandor had faced since its war with the giants, and none were trained to combat it but the old and the ageing who could barely conceive or imagine, let alone understand, what they would be up against.

And where were the seers of the future? she wondered. Where were the mages? Where were the wanderers who would take the place of Kadmon and Gerwyn? Where was the one who would replace the elf mage departed to the sunset isles? There were other bright stars in the crying pool that had yet to be linked to Seers' Keep. And again, when she looked at them, Carrie saw their faces: a girl minding goats on an unknown hillside, a youth serving in a tavern, a dwarf maiden singing as she stirred a cauldron of soup, an elf in a punt on the River Avar, a young orc hauling in a fishing creel. But why weren't they here? thought Carrie. Why weren't they here, now, in this council chamber, along with their elders? She turned to the Enchantress.

"Where are the others?" she asked.

"What others?" said Merganna.

"The younger ones," said Carrie, "The seers and mages of the future? Those whose faces I can see in the scrying pool."

In the dim light Merganna frowned.

"You have a strange imagination," she said brusquely. "Those who show any promise are already here in Seers' Keep, or else being tutored elsewhere. And I see no one in the pool. No one at all, Carrie."

And she did not want to see, Carrie realised. None of them did. They would have to see the truth of themselves first, know that their time here was almost done and be prepared to relinquish their power and their places. They had had centuries to train the next generation, but none had been raised to their level, none sat with them in this council chamber, not one single younger voice had been admitted to speak among them.

The dwarfs were right after all, it seemed. The seers ruled this land just as surely as the giants had ruled it before them, although their intentions were benign. They ruled in secret, ruled with kindness, but as with their predecessors they would not give up and nor would they move aside, not even for their own successors. Engulfed in magic, their vision veiled by enchantments, they failed to recognise the necessity, stayed blind to the truth that the Black Mage had revealed.

Small wonder, thought Carrie, they had considered Kadmon's loyalty to be suspect. Small wonder the gasp of consternation when his shade had appeared in their midst. Had he lived he would have brought them down, every last one of them, confronted them with what they were and forced them to accept.

And now there was only Carrie who knew the truth, a girl from another world who had followed Roderick through a portal and entered Llandor by mistake. Or maybe not? The seers kept the portals closed, Garriel had said. But the land called who the land needed, and progress, of the material kind, was probably inevitable. Eventually, with or without Craig's help, things would begin to change as surely as they had done in Carrie's world. The inventiveness of human beings could not be stoppered for ever and the knowledge stored at Seers' Keep would someday seep out. Someday the powers of seers and mages would be replaced by other powers – science and technology and mechanisation. It would begin in Mordican probably, the Grimthane in another guise unleashing a dark industrial tide that would sweep across Llandor, bringing death and despoliation that no one could stem.

In her mind Carrie could see it, but who was she to tell them? Her testing was over. The pool at her feet turned dark, and the seers and mages rose from their seats with a rustle of robes, preparing to leave the chamber. Later, perhaps, they would discuss her and arrange for her to be tutored, and then they would forget about her for the next fifty or a hundred years.

"Come," said Merganna.

"Wait!" cried Carrie.

The seers paused.

And her voice echoed. "Please! You've got to listen!"

"You speak out of turn," Merganna said gently.

"But you don't understand!" cried Carrie. "You don't know what's going to happen! You've got to listen to me now and start preparing!"

"Your time will come to address the council—"

"By then it could be too late!" Carrie said

frantically. "And the future is ours! Ours not yours! You won't be here, will you? None of you can live for ever! And it's not enough to teach us! You have to let us in! You have to let us share! If the Grimthane has Craig then the rules are going to change and it'll be us who'll have to fight the next battle! And where are we? Where are the ones who will take your places? Why aren't they here?"

"We *are* here, some of us," Gwillym said softly.

"We're right behind you," said Janine.

"Where we shall always be," Bannock said stoutly.

"At your service, my lady," Garriel announced.

"Even me," said Jerrimer.

Slowly, barely able to believe her ears, Carrie turned round. Unseen, unheard, they had crept in to join her, the companions of her journey, none of them lost, none of them dead. They had met up in Scurry, Gwillym said. He, Janine and Jerrimer travelling by cart from Irriyan, Garriel and Bannock returning there with Elvertine from the desert. They had sailed together on the *Sea Sprite* and disembarked at Seers' Keep not half an hour since. But their stories could wait, along with Carrie's own. It was enough that they were there, enough that they were with her and would stand by her, enough that she was no longer alone.

The council hall turned wild, rang with their

voices and Carrie's laughter, the seers, the mages, the Grimthane and the threat to their future temporarily forgotten. Old eyes frowned down on them, shocked by the intrusion and the lack of decorum, as they danced and capered around the scrying pool.

Merganna frowned, too, and remembered. Once, she had been as they were – young, passionate, her life still before her. Once, when Merrigan staged an uprising and fled from Seers' Keep and the giants were driven from the land, she had danced as they danced now round this same pool, and loved the land as they loved. With that love she had bound the others to her, to work with her in the aftermath of war, to bring about a settled peace, establish order from chaos, defend and protect the land from the Grimthane's encroaching evil. They had named her the Enchantress – but that was long ago, and long ago her work had been completed.

Her green gown shimmered as she crossed the floor and opened the great arched doors to let in the light. High above, a bird cruised the thermals on still wings, a scrap of darkness casting a tiny shadow on the land beneath it. It was an omen of the future, and its shadow would grow. But it was not Merganna's future, not her fight. The time had come to do as Kadmon once said she must, relinquish to another her power, her position and her place. Turning,

Merganna let go of her magic. She was what she was, an old woman now, as were they all, old seers and old mages. But the land had called who the land needed: three elves and a dwarf and Gwillym the Mapper, faces in the scrying pool she had chosen to ignore, and a human girl wearing a russet gown – Carrie from the other world, the next Enchantress.

Catching her eye as she came towards her, Merganna was not too proud to smile.